OUTLAW LADY

Spur decided it was time for a quick chat with the girl in room 714. He hurried up the stairs, went directly to the door and knocked.

"Yes, what is it?" a woman's voice asked.

"Telegram, miss," he said.

"Slide it under the door."

"I can't. You have to sign for it."

He heard the door unlock and it opened a little. He started to hand her the telegram, but dropped it. She reached for it, missed, and when she straightened up, Spur saw the flashing, brilliant facets of the large Star of Pretoria diamond on a gold chain around her neck.

"Sorry," he said.

Her eyes blazed at him. "You clumsy, stupid . . ." She saw him staring at the diamond. Quickly she brought her other hand from behind her back. It held a short-barreled revolver. She motioned with the gun. "Get into the room quickly! Now!"

He stepped inside.

Hilda Johnson shook her head. "I should have known better than to open the damned door. Now what the hell should I do?"

"You could give me the diamond to start with," Spur suggested.

She lifted the weapon until it pointed directly at his chest. "I should shoot you dead, tear my robe half off and scream that you were trying to rape me. It would work—don't you think it wouldn't!"

Also in the *Spur* Series by Dirk Fletcher

#1 HIGH PLAINS TEMPTRESS   1123-9
#2 ARIZONA FANCY LADY   1125-5

SPUR #3

ST. LOUIS JEZEBEL

Dirk Fletcher

LEISURE BOOKS   **NEW YORK CITY**

A LEISURE BOOK

Published by

Dorchester Publishing Co., Inc.
New York City

Copyright© 1983 by Dorchester Publishing Co., Inc.

All rights reserved
Printed in the United States

CHAPTER 1

She was beautiful. The guard outside the building stopped and gawked at her like a country boy. The lady's tight, silky orange dress swept the ground, accenting her flaring hips and tiny waist. Above the bodice swelled full, voluptuous breasts. She smiled at the guard as she clung tightly to the arm of the man beside her. Suddenly she stumbled. Her companion tried to catch her but she fell, sprawling across the railroad tracks, her skirt billowing up to show sleek, stocking-clad legs and a white fluff of ruffled petticoats.

"Priscilla!" the man shouted kneeling beside her. "Priscilla!" The guard ran up, lowering his rifle as he stared at the woman.

"Give me a hand here!" the man in the black suit snapped as he looked at the closest guard. "Can't you see this woman is ill and hurt? Get down here and hold her head out of the dirt. I'm a doctor, I'll try to see what's wrong."

The guard, a towering youth of eighteen and strong as a bull, nodded and sat down, holding her red-haired head on his large thigh, as he kept staring at the display of shapely leg. He could just see the end of her stockings and two inches of soft, white flesh. The man beside the girl took a flask from his pocket and dampened a cloth, then suddenly pressed it against the guard's nose and mouth, forcing him to breathe in the chloroform fumes. The young man struggled little, his efforts so clumsy and weak that thirty seconds later he toppled over, unconscious, beside the girl.

The man in the black suit, Jack Houston, shouted at the top of his voice.

"Help! Help us someone, my wife is ill. Someone please help us!"

A second guard came around the same side of the building, his rifle at the ready. When he saw the woman lying on the ground and the big guard unconscious, he came forward warily.

"Help us, sir!" Houston called. "My wife fainted and I can't bring her around. This big one tried to assist, but passed out himself. Maybe you could hold her head while I give her some smelling salts?"

The guard hesitated. It would just take a moment. . . .

Jack Houston looked up and nodded. "I know how it is, some folks don't like hurt people—like him there. But you're stronger than that. Just hold her head so I can administer these smelling salts and she'll come out of it. She's in a family way now, and she faints quite often."

The guard put aside his rifle and knelt so he could hold the woman's head which still rested on the unconscious man's thigh.

"There, that's the way," Houston said. He wet the cloth again and stood, then clamped it over the guard's mouth and nose and held him from behind. The guard jolted backwards, knocking his assailant down, but he fell as well and when he jumped up, the man in the black suit swung the rifle. The stock caught the guard in the stomach and he doubled over in pain, vomiting. Houston's second swing hit the guard in the side of the head and he went down in a heap.

The woman on the gound, Hilda Johnson, recovered surprisingly quickly, jumped up, picked up the rifle the first guard had dropped, and stood at the side of the building. It was a large frame structure with railroad tracks running inside past two huge doors.

Houston had run to the other side and as a third guard came around the building, Houston tripped him, then slugged him with the rifle butt. Now the black-suited man ran to the main door and sloshed a gallon of coal oil on the wood and rail ties. Then he set it alight. The fire blazed up at once and from inside the building he heard a cry of alarm. Jack Houston ran to the far side of the building and as he had expected, the fourth guard came running around the corner. Houston swung the rifle like a club, surprising the man, and broke the guard's arm. He jolted the rifle from his hands and kicked him hard along the side of the head as he went down. The fourth guard lay dead to the world as the fire burned.

Houston ran back to the doors. "Fire," he yelled. "Fire! Open this thing up, get that car out of there!"

He sloshed another can of coal oil on the flames so they spread under the door to the inside. He heard some pounding. Then he lifted the big bar on the door, and at once he heard the inside bar come off. The doors swung wide and the baggage and mail car nudged the door. One man high on the front of the car had turned the big wheel, loosening the brake and, as Jack knew, the tracks slanted down a slight grade here, and the switch a hundred yards ahead was open so they could get on the main siding. Jack shot the brakeman dead on the top wheel.

7

One guard rushed out on each side of the car, carrying repeating Remington rifles. The car edged out of the building, over the flames, and then the inside guards saw the men on the ground.

Jack smiled and shot the man nearest him with the captured rifle, putting a bullet through his chest, grabbing the repeating rifle from his hands before he fell.

On the other side of the car, Hilda Johnson smiled innocently as long as she could; then the guard facing her frowned. He gasped when he saw the fallen man just ahead. She pulled out the pistol from behind her back and shot him in the stomach, kicked him aside and reached for the railroad car's iron handle. She ran forward and jumped onto the car, holding on as it began picking up speed. Hilda saw Jack jump on the other side, waving the rifle at her. She handed her large reticule to him as they felt the car moving faster. Soon it was at a walking pace, then a horse trot.

"So far, so good," Jack Houston called softly. He took from her bag three smoke bombs and climbed to the top of the car, pryed off the vent covers and, after igniting each of the smoke bombs in turn, dropped them down the vents into the car below.

Hilda watched the sides of the tracks. They had figured the car would roll about a mile along this section of siding before it came to a halt on the slight upgrade. By then their work must be done. They passed buildings, feed lots, houses.

There were three doors on the baggage car the guards inside could open; the front, the rear or the big one on the side. She guessed it would be the side. Even as she thought it, the door beside her slammed open and a man clawed his way out, his hands rubbing his eyes, his face black from the smoke, gasping for clean air. She tripped him and pushed him off the train.

The second man had gone out the rear door and Houston slapped him on the side of the head with his pistol, then propped the door open. The draft from the open front door now blew through the car, forcing the black smoke out the back, clearing it in two minutes.

Houston ran inside the car as soon as possible, located the safe and began twirling the dials. An old Jeffers safe—it shouldn't be used anymore. He could open it in three minutes flat, he figured. It took him nearly five until he heard the last tumbler fall into place and turned the handle. After pulling open the heavy door, he found the red velvet case on the first shelf of the safe, which held nothing else. He opened the case, saw the gem nestled against its crushed velvet, sparkling in the dim light. Houston slid the case in his inside pocket, closed the safe and twirled the dial, then ran to the front of the car.

The girl looked at him expectantly.

"I have it. Let's get out of here!"

"Give it to me. You know the agreement." Her eyes were cold and he knew she'd kill him if she had to. He handed her the velvet case, she checked inside, then smiled and pointed ahead.

"Good timing. There's the carriage I got this morning, and a horse for you."

That was the first time he noticed that she no longer wore the orange dress. It lay at her feet and she now had on a modest black gown, covering her from ankles to throat. The red hair was gone as well, and her own dark locks fell to her shoulders. The two stepped off the slowly moving rail car and hurried to the waiting rig. She looked around but saw no one close enough to recognize them. He handed her into the buggy, paused a moment, then mounted his horse and rode away.

Hilda unwound the reins and slapped them against the mare's back. She would drive on out of town another two miles to a small house she had rented. The railroad car had rolled down through part of the business section, the industrial area, and now she saw another section of residences. Hilda drove the buggy away from the rail tracks. Behind her she could hear the pounding of hooves. The Pinkertons had rallied their forces. But she would have mingled with the population before they were close enough to see her or to implicate her. She felt the jewel box in her reticule again, and smiled. The first thing she was going to do was put on the fabulous blue-white diamond and see how it looked. She had always wanted to wear a forty carat stone worth a quarter of a million dollars. For a short time she would own the famous Star of Pretoria. She wished there were some way could keep it. But she knew that was impossible.

Hilda Johnson clucked at the mare as she drove into a shed behind a modest house on the edge of St. Louis. It had been a fine afternoon's work.

CHAPTER 2

Spur McCoy stood looking at the familiar door a moment before he unlocked it, then pushed it open. Something pushed back. Inside he found a stack of mail that had fallen through the mail slot onto the thin carpet. The lettering on the door said Capital Investigations, a clever turn of phrase for the real business he was in. He kicked at the letters, papers and large envelopes for a minute, then tossed his suitcase on a chair and bent down, gathering up the pile and carrying it through the outer room into his private office. Spur dropped the accumulation on the battered desk and went through the door beyond to a pair of rooms that Washington D.C. called his "agent's living quarters."

Spur McCoy was thirty-two years old, stood a muscular six feet four inches, and carried a lean, fit, trail-ride hard, 200 pounds. He had a full head of sandy red hair, a thick red moustache and sandy mutton chop sideburns that met his moustache. His hands were hard and sturdy, a workingman's hands. Right now his face was deeply tanned and windburned, pegging him as an outdoor man.

He sat on the chair at the small wooden table and

examined a telegram he pulled from the pocket of his sheepskin coat. He had received it only that morning.

"RETURN TO ST. LOUIS IMMEDIATELY. NEW ASSIGNMENT THERE. PRESIDENT GRANT TO MAKE PRESENTATION THAT CITY OCTOBER 15. SEE INSTRUCTION PACKET YOUR OFFICE ON ARRIVAL." It was signed by William Wood, Capital Investigations President.

Spur frowned. Usually his instructions came through a retired army general by the name of Wilton D. Halleck. Wood was the U.S. Secret Service director, appointed by the President himself. Spur shrugged and went back to the desk, stripped off the sheepskin and looked through the stack of mail for the familiar manila envelope with the Capital Investigations insignia on the left corner. It was near the bottom. He ripped it open and found four sheets of closely spaced handwriting. He scanned it, reading as fast as he could, then slowed when he came to the vital part.

"Believe some group or groups will attempt to harm President Grant while he is in St. Louis. Your job to search for any dissident individuals or groups and infiltrate if possible. Your secondary mission is to safeguard if at all possible a rare gem to be displayed there during the President's stop. It is the Star of Pretoria, a forty carat blue-white diamond worth half the federal budget. It is to be put on display in the Western National Museum which the President will be dedicating and opening."

Spur looked down at the St. Louis newspaper that had fallen open on his desk. The headline leaped out at him. "FAMOUS DIAMOND STOLEN HERE!" He read the story of how the gem had been filched from triple security the previous afternoon. The culprits and the stone were both still missing and the police had no suspects.

"Dandy!" he said. Spur read the rest of the message on the lined yellow paper General Halleck always used, pushed it aside and stretched. The long train ride had left him stiff, sleepy and grumpy.

He sorted through the rest of his mail, read three more telegrams on his desk from his Washington boss, and put the official messages in the locking drawer. Spur checked his gold pocket watch and saw it was only two P.M. He pushed the rest of the mail into a desk drawer, shaved quickly in the basin in the kitchen, and adjusted the low-crowned brown hat with the sides curled upward, then headed for the St. Louis Police department. Sgt. Benson would tell him everything he knew about the case. Benson was one of the few in town who knew that Spur McCoy was a U.S. Secret Service Agent, that he worked for the government and usually did his duty undercover.

This time Benson wasn't much help. They talked in a small café across from the city jail.

"It's all in the papers," Benson said. "We don't have one shred of evidence. They went through the three-level security at the railroad barn like the Pinkertons were little old ladies. Suckered them in, clubbed them, then started a fire and shot the last three men inside. Slick, professional."

"No clues at all?"

"Sure, a red wig and an orange dress. We know the woman wasn't redheaded and doesn't usually wear orange." Benson laughed and shook his head. "Heads are about to topple over this, Spur. Anything you can do. . . ." He paused. "This a government case all of a sudden?"

"Close, Benson, too damn close. Thanks. I think I'll look over that railway barn and the car itself."

He checked over the land, the barn, then the railway car. The red wig could have come from anywhere, and so could the orange dress. Pinkertons! They should stick to bank robberies.

He almost missed it in the car. There were no jimmy marks on the safe, it wasn't blown up, peeled or drilled. It had been opened by using the combination. Either someone had sold the combination, or the man who opened it was an expert. A safe-cracker and an actress. The girl had done a good job, even to pulling her dress up, showing her legs to distract the guards. And the chloroform. He had used it before. Spur could get some data from the home office, but by then it might be too late. A safe-cracker and an actress—not leadership roles, which meant they were working for someone. He thought about it all the way back to his office. What might tie the two things together, the stolen diamond and the President's visit? *Were* they tied together?

On his way back to his rooms, he stopped to visit an acquaintance of his, Wilfried Martens. Martens was a gemologist, a diamond cutter by trade, a jeweler by necessity. He glanced up at Spur with the eye that was free of the jeweler's loupe, and the blood rushed out of his face. The loupe dropped out and he stood, his hand shaking as extended it.

"Ah, Mr. McCoy. The laughing Irishman." One eye twitched. Spur had never seen Martens so nervous, so shaken.

"Martens, you old stone cutter! Hope business is good. I have a quick question. Friend of mine wants to invest some money and I told him diamonds. He's thinking gold. Any advice?"

Martens wiped sweat from his bald head. "No problem, diamonds are by far the best investment. Gold, poof, who knows? But diamonds last forever, always go up in value."

"Just about what I told him. He'll probably have to

come by and talk to you. His name is Willy Smith. I'll try to get him over here. Thanks." Spur gazed at the glass display case where a few diamonds sparkled. "Just as soon as I can afford it I'm going buy one myself, as a start." He waved. "Thanks, Martens." Spur went out the door and walked away.

The man had been so nervous he could hardly talk. Why? He was an expert diamond cutter who had come from Antwerp to do some special work for one of the big industrial millionaires, and had decided to stay. That was ten years ago. Now he looked as if he had just put his wife through a meat grinder and was serving her for supper in a meat loaf to her best friends.

Spur watched the shop from halfway up the alley across the street, but saw no one come in or go out during the hour before closing time. Then the shade came down over the door and the establishment was closed.

Spur thought about it as he walked the last few blocks to his hotel. Could Martens be so worried because he had the missing Star of Pretoria in his shop? Under the counter, maybe, getting ready to work on it? Work, what work? It was already cut and polished, a forty carat wonder with seventy-four facets and worth somewhere from a quarter of a million to a half million dollars, depending who wanted it the most.

Spur went to his office, which he entered through a business firm entrance on 12th street. The building backed up to the Grand Hotel on 13th. The government had persuaded the owners of the hotel to cut a doorway from room 307 into the building directly behind which was room 307 in the business structure. Room 307 was Spur's Capital Investigations office. By opening the adjoining door, he entered a two-room suite in the Grand Hotel. There he had maid and room service, even hot bath water. The government leased both spots. It gave Spur the ability to go into his office and appear never to come out, or into the hotel room and vanish out the other doorway.

He utilized the hotel services now for a hot bath in the third floor bathroom, then went to the dining room for a steak dinner, and back to his quarters. There he put on his black suit and gloves, took a set of lock picks and skeleton keys, and walked into the alley behind Wilfried Martens' jewelry shop. The lock on the door was simple, and he caught the small trip alarm at the top of the casing before it closed, ringing the bell. For a half-hour he examined, prowled and searched the entire shop. He found no diamond larger than one carat, even in the safe, and there were no large stones of any kind that were being cut or polished. Perhaps he had been wrong about Martens. Still, it struck a response in him. He would watch the store the next day. There was time. The President wasn't due for thirteen days yet.

McCoy had been careful inside the shop. No one would be able to tell that he had been there. Back at his hotel room, he discovered that the strain of the train ride and the break-in had left him exhausted. He stripped and fell into the soft bed for the first time in over two months. It was good to be home.

As he drifted off to sleep, he remembered one of the telegrams he had read quickly. Ten agents were coming with the President. Something else—what was it? Vaguely he touched on it just as sleep settled over him. Something about a courier coming, bringing him special intelligence information about resurgent Southern hostility, about some group called Friends of the Confederacy. What else? The courier would become his assistant on this case. Assistant? It was a one-man office, he didn't need any damn greenhorn assistant! On that pleasant note, he drifted off to sleep.

When morning came, Spur shaved, made coffee and downed the first cup before he went into his office. He had just put down some notes on a pad of paper when he heard a knock at the door. His watch showed it was only 7:45. He opened the panel and looked down at a small, dark-haired girl he figured must be only a few days over eighteen years old.

"Yes?" he said.

"Mr. McCoy? Spur McCoy, agent for Capital Investigations?"

He nodded.

"Good. I have a package for you."

She gave him a manila envelope and he thanked her. She closed the door, staying inside.

"Was there something else?" he asked.

"Yes, I'm from Washington. I'm your new assistant on this case. Didn't Mr. Wood tell you?"

Spur stared in shock and wonder. "He said something about a courier . . . oh, my God! *You*? A slip of a girl is going to help me?"

"I've had the training. I've done courier work for six months. This is my chance to get into the field."

"A woman investigator, a woman *agent*? Damn, that's just what I need!"

"My father was a sailor, then a captain, Mr. McCoy. I can swear stronger and longer than you can. Sailors do it best." She grinned and he shook his head and grinned back.

"It just won't work, Miss. . . . "

"Oh, golly. I forgot. Here's my personnel file. My name is Fleurette Leon. My papa was French and my mother is American, and now papa has his citizenship papers too. You can call me Fleur if you want to."

"Miss Leon, it just won't work. My quarters are small and cramped. It's a dangerous assignment. Three men have been killed already. I couldn't take the responsibility. . . ."

She wasn't listening to him. She held out her file.

"Take this and look through it, Mr. McCoy. I think you'll see that I am qualified."

He reached for the file folder. This was merely an annoyance, a small problem. He'd get on the telegraph this morning and have it all worked out.

As Fleurette gave him the envelope, both hands darted out, grabbed his wrist and jerked him toward her. In total surprise he found himself plunging forward, where he struck her hip and flipped, all six-four of him, head over heels and crashed onto the floor. He shook his head and looked up into the twin muzzles of a Deringer.

"I usually load the first chamber with buckshot and the second one with a single ball, Mr. McCoy. Shall I shoot out the window for you or is this enough of a demonstration?"

He held both hands up and his shock had turned into amusement as he laughed, shaking his head. Suddenly his right hand lashed out, slapping the Deringer from her hand. It went off when it hit the floor, blasting buckshot into the wall.

His own vest gun now covered her.

"If you're going to play the game, learn to play it right. Don't ever trust anybody you point that thing at; otherwise, you're dead."

"You were so fast!"

He looked at her again—maybe five-three, shapely, slender with a delicious smile and sparkling black eyes. He sighed. A woman assistant. "Get your piece and reload it. I don't want you running around here half-armed."

"Then I can stay?"

"Willy Wood says you stay, you stay. Just keep out of my way and don't ask a lot of damn fool questions."

She nodded, then grinned. It was infectious and soon he was grinning too. What the hell had he let himself in for?

CHAPTER 3

Spur McCoy had left Fleurette at the office to sort through the mail and pick out anything important. Then he told her to check on ten or twelve of the best places in town to buy red wigs, and see if they remembered selling one to a smallish woman about twenty to twenty-five years old during the past week. It was strictly busy work, but it sounded important and would keep Fleurette out of his hair for a few hours.

At nine o'clock he put on his coat and went to watch the diamond cutter. He didn't know where else to start. The fact was, there *was* no place to start. If you're looking for cheese, you start with the cow.

He found a small café across from the diamond merchant and three doors down. He got a window table, bought a newspaper and ordered a pot of coffee and two cinnamon rolls. He could make that last all morning. Promptly at nine o'clock the shade was rolled up and Spur caught a glimpse of Martens as he unlocked the door. At nine fifteen a woman entered the store, talked with Martens for a few minutes, then took off her coat and went behind the counter. Spur used a small pair of binoculars and watched. The girl was a brunette, maybe five-two or -three, and between eighteen and thirty—how in the world did you tell these days? The woman fit the general description of the woman a hobo had seen get out of the baggage car a mile away from the train barn. It was a starting point.

The waitress came and asked him if he wanted more breakfast. He told her he didn't, and went back to watching the storefront. As the morning wore on, the girl seemed to be taking care of the few customers who came in, while Martens bent over his bench toward the back of the shop. Spur could just see part of him over his partition. The girl seemed concerned with his work, and spent much of the time looking over his shoulder.

She was there most of the morning and left at 11:30. Spur followed her, using a lot of doorways, business entrances, and sidewalk vendors as protection. She didn't seem to notice him and went into a small flat some fifteen blocks away. The number on the door was four—first unit, ground floor in front. He made a note of it and went back to his office.

Spur looked at the mail Fleurette had laid out in neat piles on his desk. One stack had a note on top that said, "throw out" another said, "read" and the last, a single telegram with today's date said, "Important!" He read it. It was a two-pager from William Wood, the big boss. In effect, it said there was some conjecture that the St. Louis diamond theft they had just heard about in Washington, was a part of a plot to harm the President. The chance existed that the thieves might be planning on selling the diamond to obtain funds to further their efforts. The last line laid it out.

"At all costs, capture the persons who stole the diamond as quickly as possible to help prevent financing any plot against the President and against the Union."

He put the telegram aside and sighed. At once he was on his feet heading out the door. The hotel side was closer. He ran out the door, swung it closed and bolted down the hall to the stairs.

Once outside, he hailed a hack and rode to the address where he had followed the girl. No time for finesse now. He pounded on the door.

A short, squat woman with her hair tied up in a bandana answered.

His frown preceded a snort of displeasure.

"I told you before, they. . . ." She stopped. "Oh, you be another one. You be hunting the couple what lived here. Brother, they ain't here now. Up and left just after me lunch cup of tea, they did. Not a word, and owing me a week's rent."

"Gone?"

She nodded.

"What name where they using, if I might ask?"

"Mr. and Mrs. John Smithe. that's with an 'E' on the end."

"And you believed them?"

"Don't bust my buttons."

"Any idea. . . ."

"None. Now I got to get on with me cleaning, if you don't mind."

"Did they leave anything? A waste basket, trash?"

"You queer? Sure, trash all over. Take a look."

He did, and a half hour later, had found nothing of value. There was no scrap of paper with a name or address, no telltale receipt, nothing.

Spur took the hack directly to the diamond cutter's store. He wasted no time.

"Martens, the girl who was here this morning—she had the missing diamond, the Star of Pretoria, didn't she? You looked at it, you knew it was coming when I was here yesterday."

Martens nodded, and shook his head. "They said they would kill me if I told anyone. A man was in the back room with a gun aimed at me the whole time you were here, then this morning too." He seemed relieved to have it told. "She wanted me to cut up the big stone so she could sell them easier. I studied it and could find no fault lines at all. To attempt it could have shattered that precious stone into a hundred pieces. I told them that. Then I refused to do it. I convinced her a collector might pay big money for that stone, even knowing it was stolen. Her chances were much better that way than taking the risk of cleaving."

"I believe you," Spur said. "But you better tell the police the same story before they come to you. Now what about the girl? Anything special? A name, description? What color eyes? Any speech pattern? Is she local?

"Local? Not a chance, McCoy. More than a trace of the south in that little one. Pretty as a pet puppy, but with cold eyes. Black, deep and deadly. She carries a Deringer in her skirts somewhere."

"Southern, black eyes, watch for a Deringer. Right. Now anything about who she worked for or with? Was she the boss or was the man? Where was she going from here?"

"Nothing for you, McCoy. She was definitely the head of the show. The man was the backup gun. She is a cool one. Didn't let slip one fact all morning. I think she was relieved when I said I wouldn't cut the stone. She left wearing it around that pretty little neck of hers. The stone was in plain sight."

"Sounds reasonable. She was taunting the whole St. Louis police force." Spur stared at the diamond cutter. "I'd suggest you close shop and go talk to Sgt. Benson down at police headquarters. He'll be interested in what you say, and it should clear you of any possible charges of complicity. But do it right now."

Spur took the hack back to the Grand Hotel and paid the driver off. Upstairs in his rooms, he found the door still open to the office. A lamp was burning inside. When he walked in, Fleurette looked up from the desk where she had been making some notes.

"Oh, I didn't know if you were coming back tonight so I was leaving a message. I'm staying here in the hotel, room 707. I checked out those wig places."

He sat on the edge of the desk and looked down at her.

"I went to twelve places, and I might have a lead." She looked up. "It's not much."

"What is it, Fleur?"

"One place was a costume shop, mostly for the theatrical profession, and one clerk said she remembered the girl, and tried to talk her out of the red wig because her eyes were so dark—it just didn't suit her complexion or eyes. But the girl said she wanted it. The clerk asked for a name and address for their mail advertising list, but the customer said she was just passing through with a small show."

"That's all?"

"I *said* it wasn't much."

"A description?"

"Yes, but only sketchy. Five-feet three, black hair, black brows, small nose, pretty, black eyes, maybe twenty to twenty-four. Slight southern lilt to her voice."

"Good, that's our girl." He locked the front office door and motioned toward the other rooms. "You've seen my grand living quarters?"

She nodded. "While I waited I peeked in. That's a nice little kitchen. Do you cook?"

"A little. Do you?"

"A lot." She hesitated. "I could cook us dinner."

"Isn't that a little bit forward?"

"Hell, McCoy, I've been forward and independent all my life! If I want something, I take it. If I like somebody, I tell him. Life's too short to be coy."

She was putting up a front, acting a part, he could tell. He called her bluff. "Sure, Leon. Cook us a meal." He led her to the door, blew out the lamp in the office and lit the gas lights in his room. He hadn't paid much attention to what she wore before. Now he noticed the lavender dress, tight at the waist, flaring over her breasts in an insert of lighter colored material, and tight around the throat. The same lighter material formed wrist-length sleeves. He saw low heeled shoes peeking from under the floor-sweeping full skirt. She turned and stared at him.

"You really don't like me much, do you Mr. McCoy?"

"How could I dislike you, Miss Leon? I know nothing about you. So instead of eating up here, let's go down to the dining room. I'll need to know lots more about you if we're going to work together. We'll have time to talk."

She nodded. "Fine. Let me go and clean up some and change. I'll meet you in the dining room in half an hour."

She did. He took a table by the window and watched everyone else in the room. The black-eyed girl with dark hair and the small nose didn't appear. When Fleur came in, half the men in the room watched her walk across to his table. She wore a soft blue dress that exposed the tops of her breasts, leaving her shoulders bare. A short jacket draped her shoulders. The dress cascaded to the floor in billows of lace. Her black hair hung loose down her back and her smile was fixed and beautiful.

He stood and helped her sit down.

"You've changed," he said.

"Those were my business clothes," she said calmly.

During the meal, she told him about herself. She and her mother lived in Washington, D.C. and she had gone to college for one year before she quit to work in the government as a researcher. Since her father was away at sea so much, she saw little of him, and her mother had practically raised her single-handed. She had never had a gentleman friend come courting.

"I think I might never marry and instead be an investigator until I'm old and weary," she said.

"Not in St. Louis, you won't," he said. "Half the men in this room watched your grand entrance."

"You're making that up so I'll feel welcome, and I thank you. But I don't need your patronizing."

After the meal he walked with her up the stairs. She paused on the third landing.

"There's something I forgot in the office, do you mind?"

He led her down the hall, opened the door with his key and turned up the lights. She faced him.

"Mr. McCoy, there is something we need to get straight from the very first. I don't sleep with every man I work with, nor with every man who asks me. Sex isn't that important to me, so I just want you to know that if it bothers *you*, we can get it over with right now and then it won't get in the way of our work."

She walked to him, reached up and pulled down his head so she could kiss him. Her tongue drove into the suddenly steaming cavern of his mouth and tangled with his. Her arms went around him and her breasts pushed hard into his chest, her kiss hot and eager now, devouring him, their tongues locked in mock combat.

When the fiery kiss ended, she beamed at him, caught his hand and led him to the bed. She undid a few buttons in front and the bodice of her dress slid down, leaving her full breasts covered only by a transparent chemise.

He stared at her, felt the furious, boiling blood surging into his male member, sensing its engorgement, bearing the sudden sharp, torturing pain of desire that seared through his pulsating erection.

She held out her arms and he sank to the bed beside her. Tears spilled from her eyes and crept down soft cheeks. His hands touched her breasts and she moaned, pressing against him. Her eyes closed, she leaned on him, then her fingers pulled the chemise away from her breasts. She shuddered, gasped for breath.

"Yes, oh, yes!" she whispered. She caught him and pulled him down on top of her on the bed. He caressed her, feeling the nipples rise, hard and ready, sentinels of her rising passion. Her hips squirmed against his thigh, as she moaned, soft, small sounds expressing her feelings, desires and needs.

Suddenly she pushed him away and sat up, then turned her nakedness away from him.

"No." she said softly, fiercely. "No, Spur! I can't do it, not this way. I lied to you. All that frank talk about taking what I want, about going to bed with some of the men I've worked with?" Her hands hid her breasts, arms crossed as she turned to him. "Spur, I've never done it. I've never even come close. I'm a virgin, Spur." She looked at him and the tears came again. She started to brush them away, then she shrugged, wiped at them and lowered her hands.

"Oh, God, but you're beautiful, Spur McCoy! I'd rather my first time was with you than any man I've ever seen. Then you can send me packing if you want. Will you make me into a real woman?" She caught his hands and brought them up to her breasts. The heat of them seemed to scorch his hands as he caressed them, making the ripe pink buds grow even larger. She leaned over then, fell against him, and lay across his legs, her bare breasts staring up at him like two pink eyes. Her lips were slightly parted, her eyes devouring him with urgent desire.

"Spur, no man has ever touched my breasts before. It gives me a delicious feeling I've never known. It sparks wonders and delights I've only dreamed about!" She lifted herself up and pushed him flat again, crawling over him, pulling the dress down, gently lowering one full, pink-tipped breast to his lips. He kissed it. She groaned in delight, then her nostrils flared, her whole body shivered and a sudden look of total awe flashed in her eyes. She trembled as if caught in an earthquake. She pushed her breast against his lips until they opened, then her marvelous smile came and spasms of total sexual pleasure convulsed her body as she closed her eyes and fell against him as the climax thundered through her. His mouth tasted the morsel, gulped in as much as he could and caressed the hard nipple with his tongue.

When the last tremor slashed through her, she looked down at him in awe. Her eyes were like saucers.

"Oh, Spur, I've never. . . ." she gasped for breath. "I've never in my life felt . . . felt . . . experienced . . . anything like that! Oh, gracious!" She pushed back a little so she could focus on his face. Then she bent slowly and kissed his lips with a humming bird's wing brush. It was so sweet and tender, that Spur wanted to tell her. But he looked at her and she knew. He didn't want to break the spell.

"Darling Spur." She hesitated. "May I call you 'darling'?"

He nodded. Spur had deflowered a few maidenheads in his time, and he understood the importance women attached to it. Each must go at her own pace, and sometimes they never made it all the way on the first try. Patience.

"Darling Spur, I just can't ... I don't have the words to say what I feel. Such emotion!" She blinked back tears. "It's more grand than I ever dreamed, ever hoped. And I know we're just beginning."

She unbuttoned his jacket, them pulled off his tie and undid the buttons on his white shirt. She rubbed his bare chest and the reddish hair on his chest.

"Everything is just perfect." She sat up and cupped her breasts, lifting them. "Although *she* is jealous." Fleur pointed to her left breast. Spur leaned up and kissed it, then his tongue caressed the elongated nipple and at last he bit it tenderly. She gasped, then her arms came around him and she kissed his neck.

"Darling Spur! Would you help me out of this damned dress?"

He did, working it up over her head, then removing the lacy chemise under it, leaving her bare to the waist. He was suddenly engulfed in a sea of petticoats. He brushed them aside and looked at her.

"Soon," she said. She helped him take off his jacket and then his shirt, and marveled at the sculptured look of his wide shoulders, his hard stomach and the red buds of his nipples. She fingered them, bent and kissed them, and quickly looked at him.

"It's not quite the same for a man," he said. "Men get ready in other ways. Mother Nature knew just how to do it." He kissed both her breasts and she glowed.

Her hands touched his shoulders, his chest, and then the reddish hair just over his pants.

"Can you undo a belt?" he asked, then kissed her ear, his tongue licking it, sending shivers up and down her back. She smiled and touched him again, then pulled at the belt until it came free and parted. She looked at him with soft green eyes and he nodded. Fleur struggled a moment with the buttons on his fly, then found the combination and opened them. She had stared at the long bulge coming from his crotch toward his waist, and now she touched it, then rubbed it through the broadcloth.

He moved slightly and she gasped. Then the buttons were open and her long, delicate fingers probed under the cloth. Her hand closed around his maleness and she made more small, sensuous noises deep in her throat. She was breathing faster now, her eyes glistening. He sat up and pulled his boots off, then stood and motioned to his pants. She sat on the bed in front of him and tugged at them, pulling them down slowly. His underwear came with them, and in a moment they were around his knees. His erection sprung out at her and she gasped.

"My God! It's huge ... I had no idea ... oh, my God!" He caught her hand and closed her fingers around his shaft and she almost climaxed again. She blinked back tears of emotion and grew more curious, holding him to the side, examining the flared mushroom head of his penis, tracing down the long stem to the forest of dark red hairs below and the heavy scrotum.

"Beautiful, just beautiful," she said, her eyes looking up at him with surprise and amazement. "How in the world can you walk around. . . . oh, I forgot. I suppose it's not that way all the time, just when you're ready to. . . ." She lifted her brows.

He stepped out of his clothes and sat on the bed, then kissed her again. Now he could feel the moist heat of her mouth, as she scalded him and battled his tongue. His hand rubbed her breasts and he lay back on the bed, bringing her with him, playing with her tits until they were so hot he thought they might burn. Then one hand trailed down her belly and over the petticoats to her leg, where he found soft cotton underdrawers.

She gasped as his hand closed around her inner thigh.

"Oh, gracious, it's time, isn't it?" She looked at him with anticipation and a touch of fear.

"If you want it to be," he said.

She nodded, and pulled down the three petticoats all at once and kicked out of them. The drawers were white, waist to knee, decorated with soft yellow bows and lace. They were the fanciest drawers he had ever seen and he was sure she had put them on especially for tonight. He rubbed one hand up her covered thigh and brushed across her crotch and she moaned, humping her hips upward for another caress.

He repeated it and then his hand closed over her heartland and she gasped and moaned again, nodding at him when he looked at her.

"Yes, darling Spur. It's all right. It's what I want."

He rubbed her through the cloth for several minutes, until he could feel dampness. Then he rolled her over on top of him and let his shaft rest against her mound. Her eyes widened and then they calmed and she kissed him long and hotly. Her hips began to move, rubbing herself against his erection.

With his help she pulled down the drawers till they rested around her knees. She clung to him, and he felt the heat, the moist urgency of her. At last she kicked off the drawers and he rolled her to her back, his hand moving down to her thatch as he kissed her gently. She responded with her mouth wide open, fire in her eyes and her hips starting to move. She pumped her damp loins against him, pressing her heat into him. Her soft brown nest bristled against his shaft, devouring the veined erection, demanding his attention.

His hand touched her very center and she gasped in pent up anticipation. She was smiling, a beautiful smile. He touched her again, rubbing the soft dampness, searching for the right spot, finding it and kneading it twice before her trigger went off and she surged into another climax. She jolted against him this time, and his hand could do no more than grab a handful of bouncing crotch and hold on. She steamed and groaned and bit his shoulder, her fingernails leaving red welts along his arms, back—wherever she touched him.

At last she heaved a long sigh and her eyes opened. She started to say something, then he stopped her with a kiss and she sighed long and steadily. His fingers found her and he rubbed the soft, wet lips, setting her hips squirming again.

Suddenly she sat up, bent and kissed the purple head of his shaft and smiled at him. "I just had to thank him," she said, then lay down and looked at Spur.

"Darling Spur, I'm ready."

"Are you sure?"

She nodded.

He kissed her fiercely then, demandingly. He rolled on top of her, crushing her into the bed, and the whole world blazed as she returned his passion. The earth and sky ate up the fiery sun and the heat welled up in both their bodies and they crashed together in a surging tide of desire and passion.

She lay below him, soft, yielding waiting. He pushed up and looked at her: willing mouth, eyes showing love, breasts pointing up at him, tiny waist above swelling hips, and thatch of soft brown hair over moist, parted love-lips. He marveled at the beauty of her, the white purity of her body, and wondered for just a moment if he should surge ahead and drive himself into her cauldron. Then he remembered the age-old saying that a stiff penis has no conscience, and he moved toward her. She shuddered and raised her hips upward to meet him in the ancient symbol of acceptance.

He moved down, then adjusted himself and slid into her as a cry of surprise and joy leaped from Fleur's mouth.

"Oh, yes, darling!" she breathed. Her expression was one of exultation and triumph, of longing and waiting and the realization that the time had at last arrived, but there was also a touch of eager anticipation at what would come next.

He slipped slowly into the satin folds of her, felt her untried muscles gripping him, denying him a moment, then relaxing.

"Darling, it is beautiful, so sweet and wonderful!" she said, the words gushing out, unbidden, spontaneous, long awaited, as if she had been searching for the feeling for years.

He stopped probing deeper, realizing that the barrier was still there, the protective hymen barring him from possessing her completely.

She looked up. "I know. I told you. I know it will hurt a little, but please go on. Make me a real woman!"

He nodded and began to press deeper, to glide in, then out, to edge a little farther each time, to bend, to pry, to stretch the fibers, knowing they were created to be broken one day.

She smiled up at him, nodding. "Yes, darling, yes! More, more! I love you! Darling, I love you so much!" He knew the words were sexually stimulated, but it was good to hear, and like man from the dawn of time he bent to her ear and whispered all those things man has always told his expectant mate as they approach total union. And he meant them. For the moment, for the heat of the seconds, the minutes, he did love her. There was no way anyone could deny such love when he and she were locked in such a torrid embrace.

Harder—he stroked harder, deeper. He could feel the barrier weakening.

Her hips moved under him. He took more weight on his knees and elbows, and she pumped upward.

"Quickly, now, darling, or I won't be able to stand it!" she nearly shouted at him, tears seeping out of her eyes, her flanks glistening with sweat, her hips rising upward at him in a driving frenzy.

Like a range bull rutting a virgin heifer, he drove into her again, then once more and he could feel the hymen tear apart. He drove on, deep into the very heart of her, into the churning love juices.

Her cry was sharp and short, like a prelude to joy that first must mark some note of pain. But the pain dissolved in an instant and she was past it, surging, animal pleasure flooding out the small pain, drowning it. It was the exuberant cry of a young girl entering womanhood, eager for the adult rites that had been denied her for so long.

His own reaction came at the same time. First shock at her pain and despair that he had caused it, quickly shunted aside by the sexual excitement of driving in deep, of knowing that the ritual of love had started and could end only with a glorious surging climax of power, desire and joy.

"Darling Spur, I am a woman. Please treat me as a woman and make me feel more wonderful than I ever have, all the joy and fulfilled desire I could never experience before!"

Then all thought of consequence and tenderness and responsibility, all that was civilized and moral and right faded away and he was conscious only of the woman-animal under him and his own surging desires and needs. She was the vessel created to accept willingly, to help him to his own fulfillment. He pounded into her body, he filled her to the lovely brim, he speeded up, he slowed, he listened to her moaning and gasping, he felt her shudders as she climaxed two, three, then four more times as he searched for the perfect moment.

Then the purely physical seemed satiated, and he flew with her into the heavens, circled the valley, soared past the mountains and away from the sun into darkness again, then sunlight and he realized they had been all the way around the globe. They sailed to the moon. She crooned and sang beneath him, her thighs surging up to meet each of his thrusts, her voice like a rhapsody, a concert.

Then she shrieked as her eyes glazed and her hips thrust more urgently as she convulsed with spasms of yet another climax that pushed him to greater action. He felt the driving force in his loins, carrying him to the sky and he overflowed and drove into her until he was spent and his seed sown, his body going limp and she coming down from her pinnacle at the same time as they lay there, exhausted, gasping, panting, unable to speak or move or even think as the darkness of the little death swept over them and they rested.

He slid away from her after a while, turned on his back beside her, too spent to move further. She looked at him, and smiled, and knew she would love him forever.

"Mr. Spur McCoy, I will thank you for the rest of my life for what you did for me today." She was serious, then smiled. "I mean it Spur McCoy, I'll always be grateful—but I won't tie you down, and I won't be clinging, and I won't let it interfere with our work."

He watched her. "Remember, making love won't always be that good," he warned.

"I guessed that." Then she giggled. "Look at that poor little guy! I killed him dead, but he really went down fighting."

Spur laughed and kicked his legs off the bed. "Don't you worry about him being dead. He's like Lazarus—he's risen from the grave more times than you can shake a new-fangled buggy whip at!"

CHAPTER 4

The little man was troubled and angry. He stood a mere forty-two inches tall, with a hunch back and an oversized head with stringy gray hair. His eyes bulged, darting around with hyperthyroid agitation.

"I don't give a shit what you say, stupid!" the small man thundered. His head cocked to one side gave him a twisted, gnarled appearance. "Too many people *saw* you! Don't you have any sense at all? You're still thinking with your ass! How many times do I have to...." He grabbed at his chest and eased back on the hotel bed where he sat, taking long, slow breaths.

The girl was at his side at once, easing him down on the comforter, lifting his short legs in their high-heeled boots to the bed, putting a soft, damp cloth on his brow.

"There, there, now sweetheart, just relax. It's going to be all right. I told you I wouldn't lose it. See?"

She removed a scarf from her throat and the gold chain was revealed, the forty carat diamond dangling free, flashing like sparkling fire in the gaslight.

He grabbed the diamond, jerked it sharply downward, breaking the small link chain, and held the jewel in his hand.

"Beautiful! My salvation! The end of all our money problems! The man I wired yesterday should be here by tomorrow at the latest. He has offered me three hundred thousand dollars for this bauble! Then we can truly finalize our plans." He took the cloth, wiped heavy perspiration off his forehead and cheeks, and let her help him sit up.

His eyes darted to her bosom.

"Let me see your other two jewels, my pet," he said.

Hilda Johnson smiled at him. Slowly she undid the buttons at the throat of her dress, making him wait, teasing him. When she had them opened part way she paused, heard him growl and hurried on, unfastening the buttons, pushing the blue dress aside. Only a silk chemise covered her. He reached up and pulled it down, and hooked the chemise under her breasts. His hands attacked her breasts which were large, brown-tipped, with heavy nipples.

"Sweetheart, do you want. . . ?"

"Quiet, woman!" he roared. "I'm thinking. Isn't a month long enough for you to remember that? I need to play with your tits when I'm thinking."

She sat, let him fondle her. At their first meeting she had wanted to laugh at this gnome of a man, at his misshapen body, his tiny torso and short legs. But when he had been fascinated with her breasts, and when she saw how much money he had to spend on her, she began to find many good points about him. His sexual needs were unusual. He had never actually made love to her yet, but she had satisfied him sexually at least once a day. Even as she thought about it, she saw him humping his small hips and panting. He was climaxing and she wasn't sure that he even realized it.

"Yes, yes, it's all falling into place," the dwarf said.

His name was Dr. Isidor Larman, and at thirty-two

years of age he had come to the attention of the law enforcement people in more than ten states. He was wanted on a variety of charges from fraud and embezzlement to robbery and, in two states, murder, after several persons had died in two of his schemes. He had never been caught.

"When our man from Chicago arrives, we will complete the transaction. He sent ten thousand dollars by letter of credit over the telegraph wire yesterday. We can exist until he arrives. In the meantime you will *not* wear the Star of Pretoria, you will *not* show your face outside this room. Houston is in that cheap hotel on the waterfront?"

She nodded.

Hilda looked down at him as he kissed her breasts, then lifted the straps and let the silk glide back over them.

"Does it mean anything to you, Isidor, when I let you play with me this way?"

"Mean anything?" He snorted. "Who do you think you are, Cleopatra or something? You're a woman, and you do what a woman is intended to do—let a man make love to her after his own fashion. If you don't like it...."

"I'm not complaining. But you . . . you don't seem to get much enjoyment from it. You just came and I'm not sure your mind even realized it."

"Of course I knew it, stupid bitch! My mind lets my body have its small entertainments. My mind has more important things to do." He slid off the bed, his breathing normal. He paced to the hall door, then back through the connecting door into the woman's room, and returned.

"Didn't I tell you my plan for robbing the rail car would work? Only a genius could come up with a three-stage attack like that. Now the rest of the program will function as well."

He looked at a gold pocket watch on a thick gold chain attached to the small vest of his dark blue suit. "Only three o'clock? I'm famished. Write a note for Tor and have him go down to the dining room for some food. I'd like fried chicken, clams and some white fish. With vegetables and soup, of course."

She nodded, and went into her adjoining room to write the note. She looked up and saw Tor staring at her. The man was huge, six feet eight inches tall. He was muscular and well developed, but Indians had cut out his tongue when he was ten, and castrated him two years later. Somehow he lived, outwitted his captors and killed ten of them as he escaped. Now he hated anyone who even looked like an Indian. He was blond-thatched, with piercing blue eyes, and a serious expression that softened only when Hilda smiled at him. She smiled now, gave him the note and told him to go bring up food. He knew the routine. He took the note carefully, nodded and went out his door into the hall.

Hilda watched him, remembering how afraid of him she had been at first. Then finding out he was castrated, she had realized he would not harm her. She had undressed one night in front of him and he had been totally indifferent.

Back in the hotel room, Dr. Larman was making notes on a pad.

"We will have at least five different tries at him," he said, thinking out loud. "It will take much money, and many men, but the money can buy the men. Yes. And you, my dear, will be our effort number three. Have you ever seduced an important man?"

"Only you, sweetheart."

"You'll have your chance, soon, at someone even more important—but not as brilliant of course, as I."

A knock came on the hall door. Quickly Hilda closed the two adjoining room doors, then went to the other one and opened it. A man stood in the hall, turning a black hat in his hands. He wore workingman's clothes and stared in surprise at Hilda's bosom which rose and fell under the silk chemise. She watched him as she buttoned her dress.

"Sorry, they're taken," she said softly, then louder, "And you must be Mr. Trenton, correct?"

The man nodded, his eyes still on her vanishing bosom.

"Come in. Dr. Larman can see you."

Trenton walked in, saw Larman and was so surprised that he stopped. The dwarf sat on a chair and frowned.

"Yes, man, come and sit down so I can see you. You are surprised that my physical stature does not measure up to yours. That's understandable, but now that's behind us. What about *your mental* stature? What do you have to tell me?"

"My friends are ready and waiting," Trenton said, giving the agreed-upon password.

"And your friends are my friends," Dr. Larman said. He watched the man relax. "You were head of the history department at the University of Louisiana?"

Trenton seemed to sit straighter. "Indeed I was, young man. I have seen much of life, and death, and now I do what I can, as hundreds of others of us shall do when we have the chance."

Dr. Larman nodded. "I was hoping so, and I expected at least this much dedication. The will to win often means people and organizations and even nations prevail when they usually wouldn't without that special drive. How many friends do you have working with you?"

"Within twenty-four hours I can assemble eighty-five men, each armed with rifle and pistol, half with repeating rifles. Each man has two hundred rounds for his weapons."

"And their training?"

"Eight percent wore the gray; the rest have undergone training in several categories, including marksmanship, discipline, and squad tactics, positioning and fire control."

"Excellent, Trenton. We will cooperate with you as we agreed, and you will assist us in our small mission here. This is the last time you are to come to the St. Louis Hotel. You will be contacted at the livery stable you mentioned. We expect to be ready to move within a week, perhaps sooner." He frowned, wiped sweat from his forehead and breathed deeply. His body shook with a tremor that passed quickly. "How many of your men can come equipped with horse and saddle?"

"Everyone, Dr. Larman."

"Good. In less than a week I'll want to inspect one squad somewhere out of town. Set it up for a week from today, an hour before dusk." Dr. Larman stood. "Please use the backstairs on your way out." Larman gave Trenton a small roll of bills tied with a string. Trenton put the roll in his pocket without examining it, nodded and went out the door.

Larman climbed on the bed and lay on his back. He motioned Hilda over to the bed. She leaned in above him and he opened the dress's buttons down her bodice and pushed away the silk chemise.

"Dangle your sugar tit in my mouth, woman. I have some more thinking to do."

Hilda smiled and pushed one breast over his lips. She would let him order her around now, but before this was over she was either going to have the Star of

Pretoria diamond, or a big chunk of cash. For the moment she didn't care which, as his tongue licked around her engorged nipple and she groaned in pleasure.

CHAPTER 5

Spur lay in bed early the next morning, remembering. Fleurette had been good, fantastic. Wait until she had more practice. He had taken her back to her room and instructed her to get a good night's sleep and be ready for work at eight the next morning. She had agreed to anything he said.

He kicked out of bed and dressed, put on a brown suit, white shirt and string tie, stetson and high-heeled boots.

He saw the envelope under the front door just after he dressed. Spur opened the message and read:

"Spur: I've got a tiger by the tail and I want you to swing it around a few times for me. Also catch me up on anything new on the diamond. I'll tell you what we have. Meet me in my office downtown at 8 if you can break away." It was signed, Benson.

He had an early breakfast in the dining room, checked through some mail and files, but found nothing that would help him. He was at the policeman's office at 7:55 and saw the bluecoat hard at work on a stack of paper.

Sgt. Benson looked up at him over the top of black-rimmed spectacles. His frown turned into a grin and he waved the agent to a chair.

"Haven't heard about any bodies showing up around town. You been taking the week off, or aren't you working on that Star of Pretoria diamond snatching case?"

"Funny, Benson. Now, what can you do for me?"

Benson sighed. "Not a hell of a lot. We know about what we did yesterday and the day before. Only now I've got a problem, so I wanted to share her with you."

"Got one of those myself, but I don't share tolerably well."

Benson raised an eyebrow and went on. "Her name is Aurelia Funt. She's the wife of one of the important people in St. Louis, meaning he's got money he hasn't counted for years. She is the president of the St. Louis Museum Association, and her group pulled strings to get the Star of Pretoria diamond sent here on loan for the opening of the museum. Now the owners are charging her with the loss and she's about ready to wipe out my whole department. I want you to go see her and call her off."

"Call her off? Officially I can't even talk to her."

Benson stood and walked around his desk to the door of the small cubicle, then back to his chair. "Do me a favor for once. Go see her, tell her you're with some congressional committee or something, and that the theft is being investigated by the government and that it's certain the jewel will be recovered in time for the opening of her Goddamned museum."

Spur chuckled. "She's really causing you trouble, isn't she? All right, I'll go see her and try to calm the waters a little, and I'll tell her what a great cop you really are. Now, you have any progress, any facts, any arrests?"

"Same as two minutes ago. That was a damned clever heist they pulled. The girl, then the fire and the smoke bombs. We're not dealing with some spur-of-the-moment snatch or a whiskey-filled, smash-and-grab robber here."

Quickly Spur told Benson what he had discovered about the diamond cutter and the girl. Benson's eyes lit up and he said Martens hadn't been in, but he would pay him a visit at once.

"And we'll be on the lookout for a girl of that description," he said. "Especially if she's wearing the Star of Pretoria around her neck."

He gave Spur the society woman's address and the agent caught a hack in front of the police station, determined to get the call over with as quickly as possible.

It was shortly before 9:30 A.M. when the hack stopped in front of a three story frame house with a brick wall all the way around it. A curved driveway led up to the door and out the far side of the wide lot. Spur told the hack he would pay him for waiting, and knocked on the door.

A maid answered. Formally she asked him his name and his business, then she smiled sweetly.

"I'll tell madam that you're here," she said and scurried off.

She had shown him into a sitting room with oil paintings on the walls, a piano in the corner and two small marble statues. Spur was trying to figure who they were when crisp clicking heels announced a woman's arrival. He turned and stared at a tall, stately woman of about forty, with silver hair pinned high on her head, and wearing a soft pink dress with a billowing skirt. Her smile did not reach her large brown eyes.

"Mr. McCoy. How nice. I'm Mrs. Funt. I understand you have something to do with the recovery of the missing diamond?" Her smile was reserved, somehow brittle, and it annoyed him.

"Very little, ma'am. I've never seen it, but I am trying to help find it. I work with the goverment on a special matter and since I was in town, I've been instructed to help round-up the thieves."

"We must have it back for the opening of the museum." Her tone was sharp, harsh.

"Mrs. Funt, I understand the problem. I'm fully aware of your situation, and I want to assure you we are doing all we can to find the culprits."

"That's all you can tell me?"

She moved and the dress tightened across her breasts and at the waist. He was aware that under the fabric her body was lithe, supple, and surprisingly full.

"We're doing all we can. In this type of case, often police can struggle for days with no results, then everything comes together and the thing is solved. I have a hunch that's the way this is going to be. My office and the police are both working on it, Mrs. Funt, and I assure you we're putting out all the effort we possibly can."

Her mood suddenly changed, and the smile that came now was genuine, full of charm, as if she were trying to compensate for being so harsh.

"Mr. McCoy, I'm sure that you will. Would you stay for some tea, or coffee? I was just having a late breakfast. I'm not fit to talk to until I have my cup of coffee."

"Thank you, Mrs. Funt, but I'd better be getting back to work. We have to find that diamond."

Her smile was still genuine, and he was captivated by it: honest, open, friendly.

"All right. I'll let you go. But I'm going to insist that you come back so we can talk about this again. I am concerned and I don't want to be a pest. I'll get in touch with you."

She walked with Spur to the front door and when she looked at him he saw more than interest; he detected a deep, burning desire in her dark brown eyes.

"I'll be in touch with you," she said, and smiled.

Her smile haunted him halfway back to his office. Then he at last forced it out of his mind and concentrated on the problem at hand. When you can't find the needle in the haystack, his old grandpappy used to say, you get enough folks to sit in the hay until somebody gets stabbed.

He would apply the same principle here. St. Louis was too big to find one small girl and her male helper. So he would prime the pump and see if he could get them to come out of hiding long enough to try to kill him. Out of 300,000 people, he was searching for two, which was all but impossible.

He detoured to the St. Louis *Clarion,* the largest afternoon newspaper and talked with the editor for fifteen minutes. When he left he had admitted who he was, who he worked for and that he needed some newspaper front page cooperation. The editor agreed, if Spur would give him the whole story, after it was all over, as an exclusive. Spur said he would. They wrote the story and worked out the headline for the afternoon's edition.

A half hour later, back at his office, Spur found Fleur waiting for him. He saw that she had on a soft brown dress that showed off her figure well. She kept fumbling with a handkerchief and was so nervous she didn't seem to know what to do with her hands.

"Good morning," she said.

He replied and smiled.

"I really don't know what.... That is, I'm not sure after last night just what I.... Oh, damn!" She stamped her small foot on the floor and turned away from him, her hands going up to cover her face.

He walked up behind her, put his arms around her and kissed a spot just behind her ear. She squirmed around inside his arms and put her hands on his shoulders.

"Spur, I'm so mixed up. It was just glorious last night, but now how do we work together? I get all fluttery whenever I look at you."

He kissed her lips and she almost collapsed in his arms.

Spur drew away and set her on her feet again.

"An entirely natural reaction, Fleur. The answer to how we work together is, long hours and hard so we can crack this case. Right now we need some things that I want you to go find. I need a torso, head and two arms of a store manikin, the thing they put clothes on in store windows. See if you can borrow one, but don't tell them why. Do you have any identification?"

She showed him a card that had been printed and signed saying she was a member of the U.S. Treasury department, enforcement division.

"Fine, use that if you have to. Get the dummy back here by two o'clock at the latest."

She scurried for the door, then stopped, found her hat, waved, and darted out the door of the building.

Spur went through the hotel to the desk, and rented another room which he used from time to time on the first floor back. He had mentioned it in the story in the newspaper. Quickly he set up room 107 the way he wanted it. He had a large leather chair brought in and a small desk. He put the leather chair behind the desk, found one of his hats which he took downstairs, and put up a screen of heavy iron in the near corner of the room, bracing it with two chairs and a dresser. He camouflaged it.

Back in the office he checked the mail, and found a letter from his father in New York which he read quickly. Things were about the same there.

Fleur came struggling into the office just before 2 P.M., her arms filled with wrapped bundles. She went back to the street for a second trip, then sank into a chair.

"I have it, all the pieces. But just what is this newspaper story all about? A boy was calling out the headline on the street."

Spur spread out the *Clarion* and read the headline: "DIAMOND ROBBERS KNOWN, ARRESTS SET."

"What is this all about? It mentions something about coming to see. . . ." He shushed her and read the story.

" 'A special informant indicates that the case of the theft of the forty carat Star of Pretoria diamond is nearly solved. Only the actual arrest of the known perpetrators is left. The job of gathering evidence and witnesses is being carried out by police and by special investigators. One of those is Mitch Wilson, who is gathering evidence now. Mr. Wilson asks anyone who saw or heard anything about the actual theft, or saw the culprits entering, riding upon or leaving the baggage car that was stopped just short of Barley Road, to come to his hotel room, number 107 in the Grand Hotel, this afternoon or evening before 9 P.M.

" 'Mr. Wilson says the case is solved and while the gem stone has not been recovered, the situation is well in hand. Wilson said his top efforts will go into finding more evidence against the perpetrators to insure a strong case and quick conviction. Anyone knowing any facts about the case or eye witnesses not previously contacted, should see Mr. Wilson today in room 107 of the Grand Hotel.' "

Fleur stared at him. "What in the world are you trying to do?"

"I'm going fishing. We can't find the robbers, so we'll get them to come find us. Basic detective work."

"And when they come they'll kill you," she said, tears gushing from her eyes. She ran to him and pressed herself tightly against him. "I couldn't stand it if anything happened to you!"

Her warm breasts against his chest felt marvelous, but he knew there wasn't time now. He reached down and kissed her ear, then the side of her cheek, and at last a quick peck on her mouth.

"Little flower, I am not going to get myself killed over a dumb little chunk of carbon, no matter how pretty it is."

"Carbon?"

"The diamond. I'll be in no danger. Our friend here will be the one who does the talking." She didn't understand. He gathered up all the bundles, gave her one of his suitjackets to carry, and they went by the back stairs to room 107. His key let them in when no one was watching, then he went to work. He assembled the dummy with the hooked wires provided, sat him in the chair and put a pillow under the torso to lift it so the gray hat showed over the top of the chair. Then they put the coat on the dummy and bent the elbow so most of one arm showed around the side of the chair which had been turned with its back toward the door.

"Oh, you mean if anybody tries to shoot you, they will shoot instead at our friend Bill Dummy here."

"That's the plan. I expect to have a policeman to help me. If I know Sgt. Benson, he'll be over here soon with fire coming out of both ears."

Spur checked the iron shielding he had set up, found he had plenty of room to step in behind it and a convenient peephole through an old draft slot. The iron was from some kind of old wood stove he had talked the janitor out of previously.

"You mean you're going to be behind that, when someone comes in the door shooting?"

"I plan on being there. We'll see if anybody shoots."

Back at Spur's office they found Sgt. Benson waiting.

"Don't you ever lock your door, McCoy?"

"Nothing in here to steal, Benson. You find anything?"

Benson threw down the paper. "The chief is crawling all over me about this. What's the idea, planting that item in the paper? It'll make us look like fools when we don't have the robbers by tomorrow."

"Benson, my former friend, you and your department haven't found a single clue. I have. You don't have a thing to go on. So I'm digging you up some suspects. If you don't want them, fine. If you want to help me, you can be a screener for me tonight. You can watch for the small brunette I saw. You can sit at a table in the hallway outside room 107 and let in the truth-seekers one at a time. And you can do it without your uniform, since we don't want to scare anyone away. That's why it's a first floor room. The killer will figure he can shoot me and then escape out the window."

Benson sat there nodding. He read the story again, and at last he looked up and sighed.

"Sorry I blew my top, Spur. Damnit, you're right. What time do you want me in the hall?"

Spur grinned and told him 4 P.M.

By the time they got the table set up in the hall outside room 107, there were ten people in line, six women and four men. Fleur had finally been introduced to Benson and now she went for coffee for those in line.

Spur had been in room 107 since 3 P.M. Fleur had

taken in lunch for the two of them and Benson had looked at Spur's setup before he left to change. He nodded.

"Should work, provided I don't send nobody in with a buffalo gun."

Benson took each person's name and address as he came to the desk, then Fleur let them in one at a time. Spur figured the try would be made by a man, the girl wouldn't risk being seen in public again. He sat on the edge of the small desk as he talked to the women, made a note here and there. Most of them knew little. Some had the rail car at the wrong tracks and the wrong street. Fleur announced each person, and for the first three men he went behind the shield.

"I'm sorry, I can't let you see me right now," he said from the shield which was close enough to the desk so that the first man probably thought the dummy was speaking. The man didn't seem to notice. He knew little more than the women. He was still behind the hiding place when the door popped open and he saw Fleur pushed inside, the door slammed shut and locked. The man grabbed Fleur by the shoulders and pulled her to him face to face. The invader glanced at the chair and Spur saw the man had pulled out a Colt .44.

"Don't move, Buster, or this little girl is dead, you hear?"

Spur remained silent.

"Answer me or she gets the first slug!"

Spur hadn't figured out how to nail the man without shooting him, even without a hostage, and this compounded his problem.

"I hear," Spur said.

The voice didn't fool the man. He glanced at the shield, then back at the chair. He triggered a shot at the hat that showed over the top of the chair. The crashing roar of the .44 pistol shattered the room, jolting Fleur with surprise and fear, but when he let go of her with one hand on his gun, she edged backward half a step and rammed her knee upward with all the strength she had into the gunman's crotch.

Her knee struck his genitals with pile-driving force, smashed his scrotum upward, crushing one testicle against his pelvic bones, sending a debilitating wave of screaming pain and nausea through the man who dropped to the floor, writhing in agony. She kicked his gun hand, and jolted the weapon from his fingers. He took one awed look at her, then curled into a ball on the floor, alternating screams and whimpers.

Spur jumped from behind the screen and picked up the man's weapon, searched him and found a derringer in his jacket pocket and a six-inch stiletto strapped to his ankle.

"Not a very nice customer," Spur said. "I'd forgotten how well you can take care of yourself."

Fleurette looked down at the man, her eyes wide in wonder.

"In training they assured us it would be effective. I've never used it before. Did I kill him?"

Spur laughed and shook his head. "He won't want to think about having a woman for a few weeks, maybe months, but he'll mend, and after this he'll have more respect for a woman's knee."

Spur looked outside the door and found a .44 pistol in his eye.

"Spur, that you?"

It was Benson. Spur shoved the door open.

"Heard the shot so I cleared the hallway. I'm taking statements from the rest of them. You find our man?"

"I'd say so. At least he should know who hired him. It might take a day or so of persuasion, but we'll work it out."

"I shouldn't be here," Benson said. "How did you

get him down so fast?"

"Ask my bodyguard," Spur said, pointing to Fleur. She blushed.

"*You* put him down, young lady?"

"Yes."

"And disarmed him too?"

"Right." Her reply was with more sureness, and newfound pride.

"How?"

"It's called a 'knee to the groin' in our unarmed combat training."

"It must work."

Fleur nodded and smiled. "It sure does!"

"Benson, why don't you take Fleur to help you with the statements outside? I'm going to have a little talk with our friend here."

"I want to stay," Fleur said.

"You really don't. Now go with the sergeant and help him. I hope this won't take long."

She frowned, pouted for a moment. He smiled at her and she lifted her brows and left the room with Sgt. Benson.

CHAPTER 6

Spur looked at the man on the floor. He was five-ten, a hundred and sixty pounds or so, with soft hands, wearing a gambler's black suit with a fancy ruffled front white shirt and a thick black cravat. Almost a dandy. His face gave him away. A small knife scar on the right cheek, and a jagged one from his left eye back into the hair line. A brawler.

Spur nudged his feet and the man wailed again. The agent tossed a glass of water on his face and received an angry, defeated stare from the man.

"Hurts . . . like . . . hell."

"You should be careful who you try to hug."

"Bastard!"

Spur kicked his shoe. The jolt traveled through his legs and into his crotch. A guttural roar exploded in the room.

Spur sat down on the bed and stared at the man. "Let's get one thing straight here, asshole. I am not the police. I don't have anything to do with the police. You're mine. As far as I'm concerned, you're another piece of dead meat. You can walk out of here hurting a little bit, but feeling one hell of a lot better than you do now—or you can be carried out in several baskets in small pieces, wondering how you took so goddamned long to die. It's up to you."

"Goddamn, goddamn, goddamn!" The bloodshot eyes turned up toward Spur. "What do . . . you . . . want?"

"You *know* what I want. The same reason you came here to kill me. I want the diamond, I want to know who you work for. I want to know where the brunette girl is who was with you on the heist. And I want to know all about the Confederate sympathizers who are working with you."

Silence. The man did not look up.

Spur kicked his foot again, harder this time.

"Now, let's start first with your name, asshole."

"Jack Houston."

"See how easy that was? Where is the diamond?"

"I don't know." He looked up in terror. "So help me, that's the fucking truth. I gave it to the girl. She's got it." He relaxed a little when he saw Spur would not kick him again.

"And where is the girl?"

"Look, he'd kill me if I told you. You don't know the kind of people he has working for him. I'd be dead in twenty-four hours."

"Twenty-four hours may taste sweet compared to say, twenty-four minutes. You don't tell me everything I need right now, I start slicing you into little chunks." Spur had pulled the stiletto from its sheath and showed the glistening point to the man. "You know how sharp this sticker is, right?"

Sweat slithered down Houston's nose and dropped onto the rug. He squirmed, then winced in pain. He glanced up. "You got to promise to help me get away."

"Anywhere you want to go: Texas, California, Mexico. You'll get there."

"You sure?"

"What have you got to lose except blood?"

Houston stared at him, frowning, then lifted his brows in resignation. "The only name I know for the girl is Hilda Johnson, but that's just one of her names. Right now she's in room 714 in the St. Louis Hotel." As Houston said it he began to shake. He went rigid, his body straightened and he vibrated into an epileptic seisure. It didn't last long but when the shaking tapered off, he was sleeping. Spur shook him, slapped his face, but he wouldn't come out of it. Spur went to the door and motioned for the policeman.

The agent told Sgt. Benson what happened.

"Probably some internal bleeding and a shock to his system, a double shock with the seizure. We better get him into the prison ward at the hospital and keep an eye on him. Did you get enough?"

"The girl's name is Hilda Johnson and she's in room 714 at the St. Louis Hotel. But don't pick her up. I want to use her to get us to whoever they both are working for."

"I should put a man with you."

"You should but you won't. You've got a prisoner, and as soon as he's stable, you can question him some more. You'll be a hero in the department. Get him out of here. Oh, and no action on room 714, all right?"

Reluctantly Benson nodded. "How in hell do I get myself in these situations? When the hell you leaving town again, McCoy?"

An hour later, Spur had deposited Fleurette in his office, given her some notices to copy, and told her to return the manikin. Then he went to the St. Louis hotel and talked to the manager. He got the only vacant room on the seventh floor, 702, just across from the only stairway to the top floor. He propped his door open an eighth of an inch with a chair and looked down the hall at her door.

No one went in or left room 714 for two hours. A giant of a man had left from 716 next door down, and came back to the same door a half hour later with a rolling cart filled with food. Spur stared at the cart. There were three plates in a stack, three coffee cups and saucers, and four large covered dishes and various other dishes of rolls, salads, even a tablecloth. Someone was eating in, but not even a man that big would need three plates.

Three. There could be three people in the giant's room. Or he and the girl could be on each side of the boss man, the top dog in the conspiracy. He would put protective people on each side of him, and the rooms could have interconnecting doors. If no one left rooms 714 and 712 in the next two hours, they would either have missed dinner, or be eating from the giant's food cart.

When the two hours were up, Spur went down to the desk, found the manager and asked him for names of the persons registered in the three rooms he was watching.

The names meant nothing to him. The woman's was not the one he had been given. False names. The manager brightened.

"Oh, yes, this was interesting—the biggest man I've ever seen with the smallest. This man registered as Tor Jones. Must be almost seven feet tall. The man he evidently works for is no more than three feet tall. A real midget, or is that a dwarf? His head is a little large and he has a wicked hunchback so he has to drag one leg. Tiny little man. Big man does exactly what the dwarf tells him to. There are connecting doors on the rooms."

Spur thanked the manager and went back to room 702. He had warned Fleurette he might be all night and told her to close up the office at five if he didn't come back.

None of the three doors moved. At last the big man left his room, pushing the cart filled with the remains of the dinner. All three plates had been used. Just as the giant left, so did the girl. She wore a robe, had a kerchief around her hair and slippers on as she walked quickly down the hall away from Spur to what he found out was the bathroom. The hotel had one bathroom on each floor. Spur let her stay in the bathroom for a few minutes, then went out and tried the bathroom door. It was locked. He waited across the hall, and when the door opened, he was positive that this girl was the same one who had bedeviled the diamond cutter. She kept her eyes down, not looking at him as he went into the room, waited a few moments and came out. The hall was vacant. He went back to 702 and edged the door ajar and settled down in his chair to wait.

A giant, a dwarf and a beautiful dark-eyed girl. The two must be working for the dwarf. Should he call Benson and swarm into the rooms right then and charge them with theft? It was too simple. The problem was he had no proof. Houston wouldn't testify in court, the girl couldn't be even linked with the theft. He had nothing but strong suppositions. Proof was what Sgt. Benson and his people would demand.

He closed the door and went back to his office.

When he got to his office there was a note from Fleur saying she had waited until she starved, then went to the dining room for something to eat. She'd check back later. He had finished reading her note when someone knocked on his hotel-side door. When he answered it, he found one of the bell boys with an envelope.

Inside was a message on soft pink paper that

smelled of carnations. He read it:

" 'My Dear Mr. McCoy: Forgive me for being so forward but I'm giving a small dinner party tonight at my home and I'm short one man. Could I impose on you to fill in? I know it is terribly short notice, but it doesn't begin until eight-thirty. I would be devastated if you couldn't come. Informal of course. Hope to see you then.' " It was signed, Mrs. Aurelia Funt.

McCoy put down the note and chuckled. Society! He was making inroads into the top society bunch in St. Louis. Out of the question. Then he thought about the case. There was nothing he could do here, nothing at the St. Louis hotel. He dug out a clean shirt, gave himself a quick scrub in the china bowl with water from the china pitcher, and checked his watch. It was 8:45 P.M., and about a half hour's gig ride to the fashionable Funt manor. He should be right on time, fifteen minutes late.

CHAPTER 7

Spur had assumed that the curved drive would be lined with fancy carrages and coaches, but when he arrived he found there weren't any there. Probably in back or down the street. He dismissed his hack driver, saying he'd get back another way, pushed the door bell and listened to the chimes inside. Mrs. Funt herself answered the door. She was stunning, her silver hair piled higher than before, a touch of rouge on ripe red lips. Her gown was long with a train, and it plunged almost to her waist between thrusting breasts.

"Magnificient!" he said, his breath taken away. "You look as if you're ready to greet the President himself at the opening of the museum."

She beamed. "Why, Mr. McCoy, that is the most gracious thing anyone has ever said to me. I am pleased." She caught his arm and pulled it tightly against her breast and walked him down a long hall. They turned to the right, went up a hanging staircase overlooking an immense drawing room, and then passed through a doorway that led into what was obviously a woman's apartment. It was a sitting room, with pictures of dancers on the walls, and photographs of famous theaters. A small fire burned in an ornate marble fireplace. She let him to a plush velvet couch and sank down, urging him to sit beside her.

"Now, we'll have a chat before dinner is ready."

There was no one else there. Obviously it was to be an extremely small dinner party... a party for two. He would not embarrass her by mentioning it, but he knew he wouldn't have come if she had said it was to be so private.

"Now, Mr. McCoy, tell me all about yourself. I know from Sgt. Benson that you are an investigator, and that you live at the Grand. Outside of that I'm in the dark."

"Not much to tell, Mrs. Funt...."

She looked at him sharply, a frown on her pretty face.

"Please, that sounds so formal. My friends all call me Aure. It's short for Aurelia. Please, call me Aure."

He nodded. "Yes, fine. And you call me Spur."

She smiled and again he saw deep, urgent desire in her eyes.

Spur moved slightly on the couch, but still he could feel her thigh pressing against him.

"Well, there's not a lot to tell. I was born and raised in New York City, where my father is a merchant. I graduated from Harvard University in Boston, worked for my father for two years, then joined the army during the war and served two years without getting shot."

She laughed and he enjoyed the sound. Aure was a good listener. He found himself telling her about his days in business in the hustle of New York, and then the long days in the army where as an officer he found little to do. He didn't say a word about going on to Washington, or his time spent as an aide to New York Senator Arthur B. Walton.

A maid in a stiffly starched uniform came in and

nodded.

"Dinner is ready, shall we go in?"

Dinner was served on a small balcony that overlooked the entire city of St. Louis. He stared in amazement for a moment.

"This reminds me of the view from some of the taller buildings in New York," he told her.

She smiled and they sat at a small table where their knees touched.

It wasn't until they were halfway through the appetizers that Spur realized that he was being seduced. He wanted to grin but instead played the game. She hadn't said a word about the diamond. She had a more interesting hobby right now.

"You will be here for the opening of the museum I hope, Spur. It's going to be *the* social event of the year. How many times does St. Louis have the president of the United States in town? And no President has ever attended a purely social and artistic event like this in our city."

He could feel the heat of her leg against his. She looked up at him.

"Spur McCoy, I'm proud of arranging for the president to come here, extremely proud. And I knew I could do it. You see, Spur, I always get what I want." She licked her red lips with the tip of her tongue, her brown eyes staring intently into his. "I've worked a long time to get where I am. Most say I'm the number one hostess in the midwest and I certainly am, including all towns and cities as far east as Philadelphia. I know the right people, I have the right connections and I'm not afraid to spend a lot of money to make a party, a display or a museum a success." Her knee rubbed slowly back and forth along his leg. "Do you like aggressive, assertive people, Spur?"

It was a loaded question and he knew it. He spoke carefully, but realized that her hand was lying along the top of his thigh.

"I like people who know what they want, and go after it. These days that's an asset, almost a requirement for getting ahead in any field. For a woman it's harder, but some women are now even taking over business firms and running them quite well."

A half hour later, he honestly couldn't remember what they had eaten. Her hand had not left his leg though it had now drifted to the inside of his thigh and her fingers were working higher. They talked of many things, but he remembered none of them.

She moved her hand from his thigh and caught his hand on the table, pulled it down under the cloth and placed it gently between her spread legs. Her skirt was hiked up and his hand rested directly on her warm crotch. She held it there and moved her right hand back to his thigh and moved it higher. He stared straight ahead, not knowing what to say, or what expression to use when he glanced at her. She smiled at him.

"Now, Spur, that makes it a little more even. There's no reason I should have all the enjoyment."

He was aware that the serving girl had come into the room again, only with a difference. She wore the same small white cap, and the starched white collar, but below that she was bare to the waist. He couldn't help but stare at her modest breasts that bounced as she walked. They were tipped upward slightly and thrusting outward instead of straight ahead. He cleared his throat and Aure laughed.

"Will there be anything else, Mum?" the girl asked, staring hard at Spur. She stood beside him, her perky breasts at eye level with Spur and less than a foot from his face.

"I'm not sure. Spur, is there anything else you want?"

He glanced at Aure, relieved to look away from the young girl.

"I . . . I don't exactly understand," he said.

"Tina usually likes to have at least a kiss goodbye when she's done serving."

"Oh."

The girl stepped forward, her breast an inch from his lips. Spur chuckled, bent and kissed it; then she turned for him to kiss the other one but he put his mouth around it and nibbled it.

"Thank you, Tina, you taste delicious," he said.

She laughed and stepped back.

Aure leaned toward him. "Now, beautiful man, it's my turn." Her lips came toward his already parted, and he took her in his arms and met her lips, feeling the fire of them. She pushed him back in the chair, her tongue darting into his mouth, searing his lips and mouth, conducting a private war against anything that opposed it. Her hand on his chest worked inside his shirt and rubbed his chest, and he felt her other hand at his crotch. Inspite of his best intentions, he started to grow, to lengthen and to stiffen.

Her lips pulled away and nibbled at his eyes, then one ear. She rubbed his erection and smiled. "Now, that is *much* better. For a moment I was afraid you didn't like women. There are such men, you know."

They stood and she caught his hand, leading him through another door into her bedroom. It dazzled him. His mother's room had been exquisite with no expense spared. But this bedroom was an Oriental fantasy, a seductive trap in pinks and purples, with a thick rug, each wall draped with silks and heavy curtains in the most luxurious material available.

Aurelia paused just inside, kissed him again, pressing her body hard against his from hips to lips. She come away slowly, then motioned to the door. The topless girl stood there, smiling.

"Would you like Tina to stay with us? She loves to watch, or to help out."

He stared at the girl, who was lifting her bare breasts and pushing them toward him. He'd almost hired two girls at a high class bordello in New Orleans once, just to see what would happen, but he hadn't. Now all he could do was nod.

"Good, I thought you'd like Tina." She carved two furrows in her brow. "I hope you like me, too." She led him to the bed and sat on the side. "Undress me, please," she commanded.

"I will, soon," he said. He stood over her, pulled her up and kissed her fiercely, pressing her head back firmly, bringing a sudden alarm to her eyes, but then they closed and his hands caught her breasts and he kneaded them like loaves of bread dough. She gasped in surprised pleasure. Then he turned her, found the combination of buttons and snaps that held the back of the dress together and undid them. He lay her down, still covered, and kissed the fabric away from each breast. Spur could feel the heat of her body radiating outward. His lips devoured her breasts, chewing on them, biting brown nipples until she wailed in giddy pleasure-pain. He rolled her over on his lap, lifted her dress and petticoats and spanked her silk clad bottom with hard slaps.

Aurelia Funt lay there moaning, real tears seeping from her eyes. Spur saw the girl Tina. She sat cross-legged on the bed beside them, the hat and collar gone now, skirt still in place. She watched them with fascination as her hands massaged her own breasts.

Spur stood Aure up and pulled the dress over her head. Then he helped her take two of the petticoats off. He stopped, motioned to Tina.

"Come take down her hair, Tina," he said. The girl crawled forward to where Aura sat on the bed and began unpinning the long silver locks. Spur moved her in front of the woman, had her stand on the floor and pushed one of her breasts in Aurelia's mouth.

The older woman moaned in delight, sucking and nibbling. When Aurelia's hair was loosened, Spur swatted Tina on the bottom and moved her out of the way. He lifted the last two petticoats over Aure's head and picked her up and dropped her in the middle of the bed. He saw that Tina had stepped out of her skirt. She wore nothing under it, and her sleek, trim, naked young body caught his approving eye.

He felt the heat in the room building, as he sat on the bed.

"Undress me, ladies," he commanded, and both moved to the task. His jacket, tie and shirt came off first, then Tina pulled off his boots and socks. Aurelia motioned the young girl back as she unbuttoned his pants herself and pulled them down, taking his underwear with them.

"Oh, my heavens!" Tina said when his stiff shaft sprung from his pants. She shivered and pushed one hand between her own legs.

"Yes, yes, yes!" Aure said. "I think we're going to do just fine." Her hand caught him and stroked the hot, turgid flesh, then she bent and kissed the very tip and Tina squealed in delight. He caught the older woman's breasts, aware that they were firm, solid, and larger than he had figured at first. They swung over him when she came up and lay full length on his body.

His hands touched her silk underdrawers and together they worked them down with her still over him, then she kept her legs tightly together and lay on him again, smothering his erection, letting it press against her hot belly. He watched her as her eyes closed and her smile broadened when his hands found her nipples again and worked them from side to side, massaging them faster and faster.

Tina sat beside them now, her finger buried in the muff of fur at her crotch, rubbing back and forth, and in a moment she reached out with her other hand and touched Spur, shivering and gasping in her solitary climax.

Aurelia pushed the girl away and kissed Spur again, her hips working in rhythm against his engorged shaft. When the long kiss ended, she moaned in anticipation and lifted her hips, moved down, and holding him just right, settled forward and down on his erection, shrieking softly with wonder and joy as he lanced upward into her deeper and deeper.

"Oh, yes, sweetheart, more, more, drive it into me farther!"

That's when he found out she was a talker. Every moment for the next ten minutes she was talking, moaning, making some vocal sound.

"Darling, that's good. Oh, yes, I feel just heavenly, so marvelous! The way it slides into me. . . . delicious. Oh, yes!"

She began to rock back and forth, to surge forward and then rearward. It was almost as if she were a jockey riding a horse.

"Lovely . . . so *damn* lovely! Oh, sweetheart just perfect. Oh . . . yes. You're so huge and hard and yummy!"

Her hips ground at him, surged away, came back and swallowed all of his shaft, then darted away and he felt the coolness of the air between their bodies.

Someone took his hand. He looked over and Tina smiled, her face next to his. Aurelia was still riding him. Tina kissed Spur and he nodded. She kissed him again and pulled his hand to her breasts, then she moved so his hand lay on her crotch. He rubbed her, massaging the soft black hair, finding the wetness. His finger plunged inward and Tina gurgled deep in her throat, her lips glued to his now. He pushed in and out with one finger, then forced two fingers into her softening entranceway. Tina moaned and bit his lip. He pumped in and out a dozen times, then came away and upward, finding the tender, sensitive nub of her clitoris. He pressed it, rubbed it back and forth, and after a dozen twangings, Tina's hips bucked against his hand so he could hardly hold on. She shivered and shook and her mouth fell away from his and she rolled away to the other side of the bed.

Above him, Aurelia kept riding. She didn't seem to be to the first pole yet, just kept bucking and riding. He felt her have a mild climax and keep right on going. Then she jolted and squirmed in her own ecstasy. Her talk had dwindled to a mumble now that only she could understand. As she exploded over him the volume came back up.

"Great gods in all the heavens! So perfect! So wonderful. Yes! Yes! Forever, go on forever!" She gasped in a lungful of air and kept singing out her delight. Slowly she came down from her high. She looked at him.

"Big fellah, you still with me?"

He nodded.

"Won't be long now."

She began to squirm and pump in a corkscrew manner and he felt his heat rising. Another ten strokes that way and he felt that small trap door slip open deep within him somewhere and the floodgates swing wide as the torrent began rushing to the sea.

The pressure built and built. The pleasure of it was absolutely undescribable, no one could paint a picture showing it, no scribe could put down the exact words that would explain precisely how he felt in those few seconds as the onrushing tide swept him closer and closer to the dike that must break, that had to break, that had to open and let him flood into the sea of the woman over him.

She sensed his need and her pace increased. His own hips were bucking now and lunging upward.

Spur screeched in anticipation and delight as the whole room exploded in one tremendous flash of brilliance and then he slammed upward a half dozen times before the stars settled in their places, and the moon sailed once again serenely over the earth.

She said something, but he didn't hear her and she fell on top of him, spent, and used up completely. The three of them lay drained of any response, unable to move, not wishing to, waiting for rest to revive them.

It ws nearly ten minutes later when Aurelia pulled away and lay on her back beside him, one arm thrown across his chest.

Twenty minutes later, Tina crawled over the large bed to Spur and gently kissed his lips. HIs eyes popped open. She brushed her breasts across his lips and sat up.

"You were delicious," she said softly.

He looked at Aurelia Funt. She was sound asleep.

He cupped one of Tina's breasts. "You were a smash in the dining room," he whispered.

She laughed quietly. "It's a little game we play. It always works. Once we did it right in the dining room on the rug."

He could imagine it.

"Are you ready yet for seconds?"

He shook his head.

"It's all right. She won't care. She usually goes to sleep after one or two. Then I get whatever is left. I have some cheese and really good wine...."

He held up his hand and sat on the edge of the bed. "I've got to get some sleep tonight so I can work tomorrow."

"This is better than sleep. You ever do it Chinese style, or the Mexican pretzel? I'm best with my mouth, want to try that way first?"

He stood and began gathering up his clothes. She grabbed his pants and he had to chase her into the hall before he got them back.

Spur got dressed as quickly as he could, threw a blanket over St. Louis's number one hostess and was escorted by the naked serving girl to the outside door. She stood in front of the exit.

"Come on, Spur. Once more, any way you say. You don't even have to take your pants off."

He lifted her up, set her aside and told her he had to go. In the drive a buggy waited with a man sleeping inside. The cabby awakened at the sound of Spur's footsteps and looked out.

"Yes sir, Mr. McCoy. I'm to take you wherever you want to go. Mrs. Funt told me so. Just step right in."

On the ride back to his hotel, Spur had to admit that Mrs. Aurelia Funt could very well be number one in town. She had class, that was sure, despite her unconventional sex life. As he climbed the stairs to his hotel room, he planned what he must do the next day.

CHAPTER 8

Dr. Isidor Larman nodded to his huge companion.

"Yes, Tor, it is time we go. You bring the buggy around to the back door and I'll be there. Quickly, man, quickly!"

Tor grinned and ran out the door. Isidor lifted his brows and smiled thinly at Hilda. "That man will be the death of me yet, the way he moves." His bulging eyes concentrated on the girl as if he were undressing her. Then he shrugged. "I'll take good care of you when we return, my dear. Get some beauty rest and don't leave your room except for the convenience. You know the rules. With Houston arrested we must be more careful."

Hilda Johnson nodded and went back into her room, closing the connecting door. That was a good idea, she would have a nap.

The dawrf stared after the girl, shrugged and picked up his small cane with the solid silver head and walked out the door into the hallway. He hated stairs. His stiff knee became an intolerable drawback. But today he would not permit Tor to carry him. Today he was reviewing his troops!

He struggled down to the first floor and out the rear entrance. Tor was there with a cab, and lifted him gently into the rig, then stepped up beside him and slapped the reins against the horse's back.

They drove for an hour, to the north, until they left the town and came to a grove of trees and a few small farms. Tor stopped at a huge oak tree that had a yellow ribbon tied around it. He looked both ways, then turned to the right toward the Mississippi river and into a thick stand of butternut. He stopped the rig behind a tree and lifted Larman to the ground.

At once a man ran up with a black horse and gave the reins to Tor.

"We think our general should have a horse to ride while he is reviewing us," the man said, turned and trotted back into the thickness of the trees and brush.

Abe Trenton came from another section of the brush. He moved silently and before they realized it, he stood before them.

"Welcome to the land of the Friends of the Confederacy! We greet you and we are ready for your inspection."

Tor lifted Dr. Larman effortlessly and place him on the black horse's saddle. He caught the reins and turned the horse to face the man who had just spoken.

"Trenton, yes, this looks fine. Now, lead me to your troops."

Trenton saluted smartly, did an about face and moved off at a trot through the woods, along a trail, then into an open field backed by a thicket.

He turned, saluted again. "General, sir. Your troops are ready for inspection."

Isidor turned and stared. He saw nothing but trees and brush behind the man who stood ramrod straight.

"Trenton, damnit, I don't see any troops."

"That's the whole idea sir. This is first squad." He barked a sharp command.

From around the fringes of the brush and trees ten men appeared, their camouflaged clothing becoming visible as they ran forward, forming into a rank, and stood stiffly at attention.

Dr. Isidor chuckled. "Camouflaged, by damn! It was impossible to see them, and I was *expecting* to see some men. Or course I was predispositioned to see men dressed normally with rifles on their shoulders. Very good, Trenton. Excellent! But what if we want these men to mingle with the population?"

Trenton snapped another order and ten more men wandered into the clearing from the woods. Each carried a rifle as if hunting. On the next command the men rushed forward and formed another rank in front of the first, all standing straight and tall, rifle butts firmly on the ground at their right heels. The men were dressed in overalls, twill pants and plaid shirts, caps and hats and boots, a cross-section of workingmen's clothes.

"That's twenty," Dr. Isidor said. "You can guarantee a hundred?"

"Yes, sir!"

"I'll keep you informed as to time and place. Each man is to furnish a hundred rounds for his rifle and pistol."

"Yes sir. They are so equipped and ready. We have a double chain of communication. We can notify everyone and have them at a specific point within four hours during the day."

"Amazing. I don't see how you people lost the war."

"Some of us didn't, sir."

"I can believe it." Dr. Larman looked around. "This is a secure area, Trenton? A hundred rounds or so of rifle fire would not attract undue attention?"

"No, sir. It's part of a large holding of one of our people."

"Good. See that rock formation a quarter of a mile down? I want you to put your regularly dressed men behind the rocks, and I want the other ten men to attack them."

"A mock battle, sir?"

"No, Trenton. I want the attackers to have ten rounds each. They will fire at the rocks. Tell you other men to stay down, behind the rocks and they won't get hurt. Absolutely safe. All right, Trenton, issue the ammunition and let's get it running. Live ammunition is the only way to train troops."

Trenton frowned for a moment, lifted his brows and barked out the orders. The men in civilian clothes ran at port arms to the rocks, and within three minutes they had vanished.

Trenton grouped the camouflaged men around him, issued curt, clear orders. They split into three groups. Two attacked from converging forty-five degree angles, and the third group came from straight ahead.

The men fired and moved, fired and moved when the next group fired. The ten men worked from cover to cover, and just before the first elements got to the rocks, a scream of agony and fear stabbed through the Missouri morning air.

Dr. Larman rode the black horse quickly down the valley as the others behind him ran.

Trenton bellowed a cease fire and everyone rushed to the rocks. The man lay on his side behind one of the large boulders. He held his chest. His forehead was covered with blood where rock chips had slammed into his flesh. A dark red stain came through his blue shirt. His eyes rolled up and he wept, sobbing steadily.

"My God, My God, I'm shot. Tell Trenton that I'm shot! My God, that bullet done whined off one rock and then another one—it done killed me, damn sure, it done killed me! Tell Tren. . . ."

The last gush of air whistled from the young man's mouth and his head rolled to one side.

"He's dead," Trenton said, anger in his eyes.

Isidor pulled off the felt hat that usually covered his head and held it over his heart.

"An unfortunate hunting accident. Carry him back to the command post and see that he is taken to his family. If the man is married, his wife get a ten thousand dollar bonus. Remember, it was a hunting accident. Trenton, attend to it."

Dr. Larman jerked the horse's head around and cantered back to the point where his buggy waited. He let Tor lift him off the horse and put him in the buggy.

"Tell Trenton I want to see him," the dwarf told Tor who nodded and ran back the way he had come.

When Trenton arrived, he had resigned himself to the death.

"That was Schneider, only twenty-six, one of my best. Some damn bouncing bullet! We shouldn't have had the drill."

"Trenton!" Isidor bellowed. "Don't you ever contradict my judgment again! You will continue the training, take the body home and arrange the funeral with his family. Nothing has changed. Now leave a man in charge here and take me to the factory."

Trenton's eyes flared for a moment, then he nodded, ran to give the orders and came back quickly, mounted on the black.

"I'll lead the way, Dr. Larman. It isn't far."

They went by way of a farm trail through three fields, across a small creek and into a grove of trees to a barn. Or it looked like a barn from the outside. Inside it had been floored, most of the supports shored up and room made for a manufacturing process.

Tor stopped the buggy and lifted Dr. Isidor Larman to the ground where he walked in the door and stood with his hands on his hips. His large head twisted as he watched the work in progress.

"Are my beauties ready yet?"

"Not quite, Dr. Larman. But they will be within three days. That's still two days before your deadline." Trenton was speaking. He was still shaken by the death of his friend. The war seemed so long ago and he had forgotten how much death can hurt the living.

"Make sure they are perfect, Trenton. We will have only one chance, one 'fire for effect.' If some of the flyers do not run true, our chances of success drop tremendously."

"They will be perfect, Dr. Larman."

The small man then walked the length of the barn, climbed up on chairs and benches, examined in detail the work that was being done.

"I'm sure you are aware, Trenton, that the Chinese began using rockets a century or more ago. They developed the principle but failed to expand upon it. This is refinement of their idea and my own estrapolation. You see the four-foot long tube of the rocket body? It is filled with a slow burning train of gunpowder, scientifically designed so it does not explode all at once, but by degrees, so the small blasts will develop a continual forward thrust for the rocket mass as a whole."

He walked around the tube to the tail. "Just like an arrow, Trenton, our rocket must have feathers on the end. Only we make our tail feathers from metal so they will not burn from the heat or bend out of shape. The fins are not just three, but six for added stability and accuracy of flight."

At the front of the rocket he watched as a workman laid thick sticks of dynamite in rows inside the nose section.

"Place those precisely as the diagram shows. We want maximum dispersal." He pointed with delight as the thin shell that would surround the dynamite.

"This hollow space will be filled with scrap metal—nails, jagged scraps, anything we can find to form a potent grapeshot effect when the rocket explodes." He looked at it and walked to the other side.

"Beautiful isn't it? And here is the *coup de grace.*" Tor lifted him to the side of the two-foot thick rocket tube just in back of the explosive. He opened a panel and carefully took out a gallon sized glass jug. The bottle was filled with a yellow-greenish swirling mass.

"Do you know what this is, Trenton?"

"Yes, sir. Some kind of gas."

"Not *some* kind of gas, Trenton—a very special kind. It is chlorine gas, a low pressure, pungent vapor that is highly poisonous! It sinks, it settles, it clings to low spots. And it kills!"

Trenton began to smile. "I had never known for sure the purpose of the bottles, Dr. Larman. Now I do. If the explosions don't do the job, then the gas will. It will completely cover the hollow where the attack is to be made."

Dr. Larman smiled. "You may be of some value to me yet, Trenton. You understand slowly, but we of tremendous intellectual capacity must simply live with this sort of thing constantly." He replaced the jug with care, put the panel back in place and pointed down. Tor lowered him gently to the floor.

The dwarf stood back and admired the rocket. It was the perfect realization of his design—over six feet long, with the thin metal tube to hold the propellant, the fins, and the two-foot-long warhead at the front where an arrow-like point would help it cleave the air. There were four of the rockets in various stages of completion. He walked on down the rough barn floor to the far end where the launching racks were finished. The rockets were like those the Chinese used: they were guided on their way by a restraining structure, that forced them to start their flight at a definite and predetermined angle of flight.

"Once out of the tube-type guiding framework, the rocket will continue on that angle, propelled to the top of its trajectory, and then decrease in speed and fly on a downward arc to land precisely on target," Dr. Larman said. "It has been worked out mathematically." Isidor knew that he was far ahead of his time. Current army men had no concept of how to use the rocket. They used it to launch a few flares, and for night communications on a rudimentary level. Stone-age thinking! Didn't they know this was a time of tremendous scientific advancement? The military mind must grasp the best of science and make it work for the attacking force.

He admired the circular cages into which the rockets would be placed before launch, tubes through which the rockets would be aimed and launched. He would do that work personally, and light off each of the fuses himself. This was no time to let inferiors make mistakes!

"Trenton, we are only beginning here. Someday these designs will be used and improved upon and we will have tremendous rockets that will lift off the ground pointing straight up, and then on a signal from the ground will turn slightly and probe into the very heavens themselves, fly out of sight into the daylight sky, and have so much power they will be able to soar all the way across the Atlantic ocean and come down in Europe!"

Trenton frowned, "Sir, there isn't that much power on earth! Dynamite could never do it, nor gunpowder."

Dr. Larman nodded. "True, quite true. Neither will be enough. But did you realize that the very oxygen you breathe from the ambient air is a powerful explosive if handled correctly? True. And hydrogen, another gas, is highly explosive. Perhaps combining the explosive forces somehow, or burning them separately... I don't know, but it could be interesting."

The small man nodded several times, then looked at the last of the four launching tubes.

"Keep these ready to accept the rockets at any time, and put the first finished rocket in rack number one. We're not sure of the schedule and it might be changed, so we have to stay flexible."

Trenton nodded. "Yes, we will."

Dr. Larman wiped a line of sweat off his forehead. The walking had exhausted him.

"Bring the rig around to this end of the barn," Dr. Larman said, and Tor walked away swiftly. A few moments later the dwarf was in the buggy and Trenton led them back to the main road. They waved and Tor turned the horse toward town.

As he rode, Dr. Larman was trying to figure out how he could get enough oxygen isolated to try to use it as an explosive. The problem nagged him all the way back to his hotel.

CHAPTER 9

When Tor and Dr. Larman left the hotel that morning, Spur had been at his post behind the nearly closed door in his room on the seventh floor, watching. When he was sure the small man was down the stairs, he followed and saw the giant lift him into the buggy and drive away. Spur decided it was time for a quick chat with the girl in room 714. He hurried up the stairs, went directly to the door and knocked.

There was no answer. He kocked again and waited, then heard movement behind the closed panel.

"Yes, what is it?" a woman's voice asked.

"Telegram, miss," he said.

"Slide it under the door."

"I can't. You have to sign for it."

"Oh. Wait a minute."

He heard the door unlock and it opened a little. He started to hand her the telegram, but dropped it. She reached for it, missed and as she straigthened up, Spur saw the flashing, brilliant facets of the large Star of Pretoria diamond on a gold chain around her neck.

"Oh, sorry," he said.

Her eyes blazed at him. "You clumsy, stupid...."
She saw him staring at the diamond. Quickly she

brought her other hand from behind her back. It held a short-barreled revolver. She motioned with the gun. "Get into the room, quickly! Now!"

He stepped inside.

"Close the door quietly and lock it with the key."

Spur did so.

She bent and picked up the telegram and saw that it was blank. Hilda Johnson shook her head. "I should have known better than to open the damned door. Now what the hell should I do?"

"You could give me the diamond to start with," Spur suggested.

She lifted the weapon until it pointed at his chest from six feet away. "I should shoot you dead, t   my robe half off and scream that you were trying to rape me. It would work, don't you think it wouldn't!"

"Then you're not going to give me the diamond?"

"Shut up, take off your jacket, and lie down on the floor. Now!"

Spur shrugged. There had been no time to move for his sixgun in his holster. He stretched out on the floor, ready to spring up.

"Put your hands in the middle of your back, and spread your legs wide."

"Now look, you're just getting yourself in more and more trouble. Why don't we. . . ."

She kicked him in the leg and he stopped talking.

He could feel her draw his six-gun from his holster.

"Hey!"

"Easy, mister, if you don't want to get backshot by a .44." She put her shoe on his neck and pushed down. "Lie still or I'll stomp you in the side of the head, you understand?"

He understood.

Quickly she tied his hands behind him, one wrist

over the other. He knew they were bound well with small cord.

The pressure was released from his neck and she walked past his head.

"You can sit up now. I want to see just what I've captured."

He rolled to his left side and sat up.

"Well, well, aren't you a pretty one. I always have liked redheads. You're big enough. Now why are you trying to mess around my room?"

"The diamond. You know what I'm after."

"I beat you to it, buster, not that it would matter. I wasn't supposed to be wearing it, and I got caught. That's why I can't let you go now that you know for sure. You the same jasper who was giving that diamond cutter a bad time couple of days ago?"

Spur shrugged.

She grinned. "Know damn well you were—big, redheaded, and built like a Texas bull." She scowled. "My two helpers are gone." She shrugged. "So I take care of it myself, up to a point." She took the diamond off and swung it in front of Spur. "Have you ever set your eyes on such a beauty? Prettiest thing I've ever seen, and I'd give my left arm to own it." She lifted her brows and her pretty face was dominated by sad, dark eyes. "But there is just no way."

She wore a long blue dressing gown that brushed the floor and opened at the throat. Now she reached for the belt and loosened it.

'I'm going to have to get dressed. I'd bet you're gentleman enough to turn your head."

"Try me," Spur said, smiling.

She opened the buttons of the robe and let it part. He saw a flash of bare thigh and dark swatch just beyond it as she turned. One pink-tipped breast peeked at him, then she turned her back on him and dropped the robe to the floor.

"Hilda," Spur called sharply.

She turned, staring at him. Her breasts were full, sagging just a little from their size. She didn't turn back, but let him take in her nakedness.

"How do you know my name?"

"I know a lot about you, Miss Johnson. Now isn't it about time you untie me and we talk this over like rational people?"

"Not a chance, especially not now." She pulled on a chemise, then two petticoats, and next a pair of white drawers. Last came a light blue patterned dress. She buttoned it up the back, then slipped on stockings and sturdy walking shoes.

Hilda found a dark blue shawl and put it around her shoulders, then stood in front of him. She held his jacket and the gun.

"Stand up slowly, and don't make any sudden moves, or I gut shoot you. Do you understand?"

He nodded. Spur stood with elaborate simplicity and stepped back from her. She slipped the jacket over his shoulders, letting it hang around his arms and buttoned it in the front.

"You and I are going for a drive." She put on a hat with a dark veil on it, pulled down low on her forehead. He could hardly tell who she was.

"We're going to walk down to the back door, go out and get into a buggy. You're sick or drunk, if anyone asks. If you make any trouble, I shoot you and tear up my dress and scream rape. You know it will work."

Spur nodded. He was sure she could use the weapon. She had showed him that already by the slick way she had tied him up without giving him an opening to disarm her. The lady was a professional. He didn't doubt that she had killed at least one of the guards when they stole the diamond.

They went down the stairs without meeting anyone. At the first floor a couple came toward them.

"Lean against me," she said. "The .44 is right in your side."

He leaned.

They went out the back door where she led him to her rig that had been hitched and waiting. Evidently she had decided she had been cooped up in the hotel too long.

"Step up and get in," she said, "and remember I'm good with this little pistol."

Spur settled back in the carriage, frustrated and furious at the same time. He had never felt so helpless, and to be beaten by a wisp of a girl like Hilda Johnson. Somehow he would have a chance; he would wait for it.

"You don't look terribly happy. What do I call you?"

He ignored her question.

She shrugged and smiled at him, then drove carefully out of the center of town, past the rail yards and along a road that led toward the Mississippi. Before she got there, Hilda turned off near some houses and ran the rig around to the back where she tied the reins and jumped down.

"You may get down now, but do it carefully. I told you I can use this pistol, so step carefully."

He got down and she opened the back door of the house and waved him inside.

"Don't worry, nobody lives on one side, and the old man on the other side is hard of hearing. Nobody will bother us."

She prodded him through a small kitchen, and into the sitting room.

"Lean your shoulders against the wall and step back two paces with both feet," she said.

He sighed but did it. She searched him, found his

hide-out derringer and a coin purse. She put the purse back, but kept the derringer. Then in his suit coat pocket she found his leather wallet. He had fifty dollars in it, but little else. Suddenly he was glad that he didn't have an identification card like the one Fleurette carried. She looked at the wallet, took out the fifty greenbacks and returned the wallet. Her hands patted up the inside of his legs to his crotch.

"You sure you don't have another hold-out somewhere?"

"You find it, it's yours," he said, grinning.

She told him to sit down on a settee, which he did gladly.

"That damn cord you used has cut off the circulation to my hands," he complained.

"Too bad." She stared at him. "You are something, you know that? Tall, not fat, wide shoulders and slim hips." She shook her head. "What a waste!" She watched him now with narrowed eyes, then her face broke into a grin. "Why not? Who is there to ever find out?" She motioned with the gun.

"On your feet, Buster. Through that door."

He got up slowly. But she was too far away to rush, too far to kick or bowl over. She was too good at her work.

"You're good at this, you know? Have you been robbing people for a long time?"

"Long enough. Right through the door. Now get on the bed, on your back and relax. I'm going to tie you up here and leave you. Some friends of mine will be by later. You struggle and it will make it that much harder on you."

She took rawhide laces from her reticule and knotted one end around his throat, leaving him plenty of room to breathe but little else. The long end of the rawhide went up past his ear and he heard her tying it to the metal bedstead.

"Hey!"

"Easy, Buster, take it easy. The more you jolt around the more you'll hurt yourself." Her hands rubbed on his chest now, and he saw the glint in her eyes. She unbuttoned his shirt and rubbed his bare chest.

"Oh, yes, nice, terribly nice. Do you like that, Buster?"

She grinned when he didn't reply. A moment later he felt her pulling at his belt. She unfastened it and leaned over him.

"What are you doing?" Spur asked, with considerable interest.

"What do you think I'm doing? I'm unfastening your belt. It looks too tight." She grinned. "And besides, I have a theory I want to check. I figure that on a big man like you, everything should be constructed proportionately bigger. Just *everything*. I hope you don't mind if I look."

"I don't see how I can stop you. My hands are tied behind my back and I'm lying on them. Now you've tied rawhide around my throat so if I move too much I'll choke myself."

"Good boy," she said. One of her hands reached up and unconsciously massaged her left breast.

She unfastened the buttons on the fly of his dark trousers and quickly pulled them open.

"Awwwwwwww. Look at him, just a tiny, soft snake."

"I'm not a teenager, Hilda. It takes more than a little fooling around to get me excited."

She moved quickly then, grabbed one of his boots and wrapped it with rawhide thong and tied it to the foot of the bed. She did the same with the other leg, spreading them wide apart.

"Now we'll see how cool you are." She lay down full length on top of him, squirming her hips against his crotch, and even through her clothes he felt her heat. She pushed her breasts against his bare chest and then hung her face directly over his. She kissed his eyes, then his nose and at last his mouth. He tried not to respond. Spur had never been tied up and raped before. Hilda's approach was all new to him.

When she kissed his mouth, her burning lips seared against his, and he gasped. When his lips parted she drove her tongue into him and he was surprised at her sudden passion. Her probe darted into every recess of his mouth she could reach, washing him, fighting with his tongue, then coming gently away and licking his lips, his cheeks. He had never experienced anything so arousing, and he felt his shaft surging with unexpected vigor. She felt it too and gave a little yelp of delight as she moved down and watched him come to life.

"I knew you couldn't resist me for long. Now *that* is going to be a dandy." She patted his growing erection and it jumped. Hilda giggled, then caught his penis and stroked it back and forth.

"I'm always amazed at how you men do that—first almost nothing then a long, hard pole ready for business. God I love him!" She bent and kissed the shaft, then licked the purple arrow-like head.

She moved then and sat on his waist as she unbuttoned the back of her dress.

"I just bet you're a man who likes big tits." Hilda watched him as she said it and his eyes darted to her bosom. She chuckled. "Yeah, I knew it. Big men go for boobs and tight holes." She shrugged out of the top of the dress, then she jumped off the bed and quickly stepped out of the dress and the petticoats. Her shapely figure was covered only by her drawers and the soft white chemise. She lay down on him again, higher this time so the softness of the chemise and her breasts were directly over his face. Gently she lowered herself until the cotton touched his face. She dropped down more and her soft breasts brushed his face.

He bit softly, catching the chemise, and she giggled again.

When Spur spoke, his voice was husky with desire. "Get that damn cloth out of there!" he said.

"Yeah, I sure will, darlin'." She sat up and pulled the chemise off over her head and Spur stared at her bouncing, full breasts.

"My God, but you've got a good pair!" he said.

"Show me how much you appreciate them." She moved lower and lower until he could lick her right breast. She let him give it a good working over then moved her left over him. Gradually she lowered her shoulders until he could nibble at her burgeoning, hot red nipple.

Hilda groaned softly as his mouth closed around her left breast. "Oh, God, but it's good to have a man who knows what to do with tits!" Her hand trailed down to her hips and pushed between their bodies until she could grasp his long hot rod and she moaned again.

"You know how it makes me feel when you chew me like that?"

"No," he said as he changed breasts.

"It makes me feel wonderful, all warm and squishy, all ready to let you do anything you want to me—no, to *make* you do anything I want you to do to me."

"I could do all sorts of great things for you if I had my hands untied. I work great with my hands. You don't now what I could do down below with my fingers. I'd set you on fire, Hilda."

Her eyes went misty for a minute, then she shook her head.

"No, it's got to be this way. But I want to make it very good for you. I figure I owe you that much." She pushed her breast back in his mouth and stretched down but couldn't reach her hips as low as she wanted to.

She pulled away from his lips, feeling them burn her breasts. Hilda moved to his crotch and sat staring at his shaft.

"God, how did you grow him so big? He's ten inches long, I swear. I don't know if I'd have room! God what a lovely, marvelous, sexy hot, wonderful monster!" She bent and kissed him then and slowly opened her mouth and took him. She murmured as she fed as much of him inside as she could, then delicately stroked up and down.

This time it was Spur's turn to moan. "You do that about five more times and I promise you a surprise mouthful."

She laughed and came away, then lay down with her hips on his, her head on his chest as she positioned herself so his shaft would nudge at her soft, warm, moist center.

"I'd do you lots better with my hands loose," Spur said.

"I bet you would. Maybe next time," She was moving then so his masculinity glided over her secret heartland and nudged the tiny trigger above it. Almost at once Hilda began to pant, her breath came rapidly, and she was moaning and shivering. Again and again she rubbed against his shaft and then she whimpered and clung to him as her body trembled.

91

"Oh, God! Oh God but that's fine! Oh! Oh! Oh!" She began to cry. Huge tears leaped into her eyes and rolled down her cheeks. She was smiling, and crying. "Oh, God, oh God, so wonderful, just a few more times. Oh, God but that's beautiful!"

He saw sweat bead her forehead, and a drop ran down her nose. She brushed it away with her hand as she stopped her motion, panting, lying on him, trying to gain back some strength. Her hand found his scrotum and she toyed with it, massaging the heavy orbs in the stiff sack. This time it was Spur who moaned.

"Easy," he whispered and she lightened her touch. She sucked in a breath and lifted away from him, then moved slightly again, downward. Her hand caught his erection and pulled it upward, pressing it against her swollen labia. She shivered, then sighed.

"Darlin', you are *good*, you know that? I never get this excited before I actually get poked. God, but can you turn me into a quivering, panting lump!"

Then she smiled at him and lowered herself gently toward him. She gave a little gasp and shrieked in rapture as he penetrated her.

"Oh, God, fine!" She smiled at him and dropped herself on his shaft without control. His lance thrust deeply upward into her.

Hilda Johnson screamed and fell against his chest and for a moment he was afraid she was unconscious. Then a tiny smile curled around her mouth and spread over her face.

"Goddamn, goddamn! I've never *felt* anything like that before. Nobody has ever *touched* me there before. I feel like I'm going to break in half, that I'm flying to the stars, that the whole world is mine and I'm taking it. God! I've never know anything like this!"

"Untie me and I can do a lot better for you. Untie

me!"

She shook her head. "Darlin', I can't *do* that." Tears came again and she cried as she moved up and down on his turgid shaft. "You know I can't let you go; just enjoy." She stared at him, and her eyes glazed and her body shook with a spasm that he was afraid might tear her apart. She shivered and vibrated and then the trembling shook her and again she fell limply on him.

He stirred.

"Don't go leaving me, darlin'. I'm just resting. I need at least one more." She came alive then, lifting almost away from him, then sliding down. She did that ten times in a row and Spur knew he was getting close. She watched him, sensed his breathing pick up, saw his face distort, his mouth come open to suck in precious needed air.

"Now you're going, darlin'. Just a little bit more!" She increased her motions over him and the up-and-down became a kind of merry-go-round ride.

Spur had promised himself he would not succumb to rape, but the longer he was was inside her, the more he felt his own control slipping. Then he was working with her, wanting it, feeling the rush start and the ultimate, killing, need for release.

Then he exploded, his hips bucking as far as they could before the cord around his neck strangled him. He surged and pushed upward on the bed to relieve his throat.

When she felt him climaxing she peaked again herself and when her body stopped shaking, she fell against him and they both panted for several minutes until their heartbeats neared normal and their breathing settled into regularity.

"Holy shit!" she said weakly. "You are my kind of man!"

"Then untie me."

"I can't do that, darlin'. You know I can't. You saw the diamond, and you'd just get me and the others into trouble."

"What about you and me?" he asked. "Doesn't this mean anything?"

She pushed upward and away from him, leaning over him, her heavy breasts swinging gently.

"Darlin', *we* are a slow fuck on a soft bed. That's it. We're dynamite together. I've never had it any better. I think it really excited me when I had you tied up. Kind of made everything that much sweeter."

She watched him, then slid off the bed and stood. "Buster, you are one hell of a good fuck."

"And that's it?"

"That, as you say, is it. Unless I decide on seconds this afternoon." She put on her clothes, taking her time, letting him watch every move. When she was finished dressing, she bent and kissed his lips.

"Thanks for a beautiful morning." She smiled, then sobered. "You stay right here and don't run away and I'll be back to see you. Maybe we can have another wild one this afternoon." Tears surged into her eyes with sudden emotion. "Damn, I wish you hadn't opened that door and seen the diamond!"

"It doesn't matter that much."

"It matters."

She went out the door and spent some time in the kitchen, then she came back to the bedroom. She looked at him and again tears flooded her eyes. She ran to him and kissed his lips, then scurried back to the door.

"I. . . I don't really know what to do with you. I'll have to go and ask." For a moment the tears came again and she turned. "Damn, damn, damn!" She whirled away, vanished and a moment later he heard the back door slam.

At once he began trying to free himself. His hands were the key. Ever since he had been tied he had been working on the bindings. They were well secured and lying on them now didn't help. The circulation had been reduced which slowed down his work on the cord. Slowly he turned to his side, flexing his hips and turning his head slightly. As he did the leather thong came across his face.

Yes! That one first. He moved more, then a little more and the thin leather thong slid into his mouth.

Chew!

He did. It tasted of tanning chemicals, and made him think of sweating cows on a long drive. He chewed. The tough leather was tougher wet, but he worked on it faster. He had no idea where Hilda had gone or how long before she or someone else might come back.

He had considered the alternatives she and the dwarf had. If she told the small man that Spur had seen the diamond, he was under a death sentence. They couldn't let him live.

Chew!

He felt part of the tough leather shred away, then more, then more. At last it came apart and he could move his head. Now he turned on his side and worked at the cord around his wrists. As he did, he sat up, which took the weight off his wrists and let him see how his feet were tied. They were not done nearly as well. Her passion had got in the way. He kicked hard at the footboard, then jerked his foot back. He heard one of the leathers break. He repeated the effort and the second one broke. He had just done the same thing with the other foot and got it free, when he heard someone pounding on one of the doors. He leaped off the bed, not knowing which way to run.

CHAPTER 10

Spur figured the sound came from the front so he walked quietly to the back door. At least Hilda had pulled up his pants and buttoned them and fixed his belt before she left. He turned with his back to the doorknob and opened the outward facing door. Outside, he looked around and saw two saddle horses but knew that he had no chance of mounting one of them. He wondered which house was the one occupied by the deaf old man. Spur saw smoke coming from the house on the right and ran through a small garden and into the other yard, then around to the back door which he kicked on. There was no response. He turned and tried to turn the doorknob with his still tied hands. It was unlocked.

Spur pushed the rear door opened and walked inside. It was a woodshed. He went to a kitchen door and backing up to it so he could use his hands, he got that door open. When he turned around and walked into the kitchen he found an elderly man laughing.

"Somebody playing a trick on you, son?"

"A deadly trick," Spur said loudly. "Can you cut this cord?"

The old man nodded. "Sure as hell can. You want me

to?" He grinned but sat there.

"Yes, I'd appreciate it if you could do that. Someone is trying to kill me. Do you have a gun?"

"Yep. Trying to kill you?" The elderly man stood slowly, walked to the cupboard and took out a knife and sawed off the heavy cord. Spur thanked him, and rubbed his wrists. The circulation wasn't completely cut off, but his hands would tingle for some time.

"Now, I thank you. Do you have a gun you'd loan me?"

"Nope."

"Someone next door wants to kill me."

"That nice young girl?"

"She and her friends."

"Don't believe it. No sir, just don't cotton to that 'tall."

"Then do you have a horse I could borrow?"

"Yep. Got one. How do I know I'll ever see her again?"

"Because I say so. I'm working with the St. Louis police on the big diamond theft. You heard about that?"

"Yep. I ain't dead, son."

"Can I look out your front window?"

"Yep."

Spur walked into the front room, but could see little. He went into a bedroom on the side and saw two Chinese standing near the back door. They chattered together for a minute, then mounted up and rode away.

Back in the kitchen, the old man had a gun out and he aimed it at Spur. "Bang, bang." he said. "Wouldn't that be fine if it had any rounds? Plumb out. Daughter don't like me to keep any live rounds for the old-timer."

"What about that horse?"

"Welcome to her. She's not too fast anymore, but

welcome just the same. Bring her back when you're done with her."

"My name is Spur McCoy, and I live in town. I'll get her back. What do you call her?"

"Horse, what else? She's in the little shed out back."

"Thanks. You have a name?"

"Yep."

"Would you mind telling me what it is?"

"Why?"

"So I can send your horse back."

"Oh. Yep, guess so. Name's Jonas. Old Jonas. Everybody knows me around here."

It was nearly two in the afternoon when Spur straggled into downtown St. Louis and put the horse in a stable. He ran up the steps to his room and tried the door. Unlocked.

Fleurette stared at him from a chair near the desk.

"I wondered where you've been."

Quickly he told her about watching the room, then trying to talk to the mystery girl. He told her about the kidnapping but not about the sexual encounter.

"She said she had to go and find out what they wanted to do with me, and left me tied hand and foot on the bed. I broke away and got loose and finally came here."

"Your friend Sgt. Benson came by, He said they haven't been able to get anything out of Jack Houston. He has demanded a police guard on the door, but won't say a thing."

"They just don't know how to deal with Houston."

"So where are we? What should we do next?"

"Next, you are going to take over the surveillance on the seventh floor at the St. Louis Hotel. I obviously can't be on that floor because she recognizes me. The trouble is, now that they know *we* know they are there, they just might change hotels on us late at night. You may have to stay up all night."

"Right. I can do it. Coffee will keep me awake." She smiled, then walked up and hugged him, putting her head on his chest. She pulled back a minute later.

"Is that perfume I smell?"

"Perfume? Of course not, unless it's yours. Maybe a little bay rum from my haircut the other day. Hard telling what barbers do these days."

She stretched up and pulled down his head to kiss him softly.

"I just wanted to do that," she said.

He held out a hotel key. "Seventh floor, not too far from the stairs. Watch rooms 710 through 714, three rooms. Keep a record of who goes in or out and when. Should be easy. You use a chair to prop your door open a mite."

"I know how to do it."

"You better get over there."

"Work as usual? Oh, there's some mail on your desk you should look at. Nothing personal."

"Right. If nothing happens over there by nine tonight, pull out and go back to your own room."

"Yesterday—maybe we shouldn't have. It's so strange now. I want to run and hold you all the time, to kiss you, and yet. . . ."

"We'll have some time later, but right now, we have a case. You're a good agent, you know how that is."

"Or else I'm learning. I'm sure learning a lot in a rush." She sighed, grinned at him and hurried out the door, going down the business office side.

Spur went through the two stacks of mail. One notice said that there would be five Secret Service men in town a week before the president arrived, checking out the hotel where he would stay and the parade route they had set up leading to the museum.

He sorted through the other material, found little that was important, nothing concerned with this case. He figured it was time to pay a call on Sgt. Benson over at the police station. Before he went, he checked through his drawer full of wanted posters. He had about forty. Far down in the pile he found one that made a connection.

Dr. Isidor Larman was the name. He was wanted for fraud and misrepresentation in four states, for conspiracy in various other states and for manslaughter in two states where his schemes had resulted in the death of three people. He was shown as a dwarf, forty-two inches tall, with a hunchback and oversize head. The description checked. The man Spur had seen today was somewhat older. It was an old poster.

Spur was ready to put the broadside away when he heard someone at his office door. But the panel didn't open. He took out a spare six-gun from the drawer, checked the rounds and opened the outer office door quickly.

Blood splattered on his shirt. Nailed to the door by one big spike hung a sliced up cat, bleeding in several places, with six inches of intestine hanging out and one eye bloody and blinded. The cat screeched in terror and pain and died. Also pinned to the door was a white envelope. Spur grabbed yesterday's newspaper and wrapped the cat in it and pulled it off the door. He left the spike there and tore the envelope away.

Back in his office he locked the door, put the bloody paper in the wastebasket and tore open the sealed envelope. Inside there was one sheet of white paper. On it in pencil was this message:

"If you want the girl Fleur back, bring two thousand dollars in gold coin. Come alone. If we see two horses we kill her. Directions below."

Spur grabbed his jacket, put a box of .44 rounds in

his pocket and took a box he had been experimenting with from under his desk and headed for the police station.

CHAPTER 11

Sgt. Benson read the note and twisted his moustache.

"It says come alone."

"I need you for back-up, out of sight and ready to move in when I need you. And about six men if you can get them."

"Sure, take the whole force. I thought we were working on another case."

"This has something to do with it. Fleur was watching rooms in the St. Louis hotel. Oh, and the little guy who lives in one of them is Dr. Isidor Larman, a wanted felon. So it is the same case. Shall we get moving? I'd like to be out there just about the time it gets dark."

"But you're not taking any money along."

"A ransom? Of course not. My company has an absolute rule against that sort of thing. Anyway, I don't have two thousand dollars."

They took four policeman in a buggy and Spur and Sgt. Benson rode horses. The directions showed the way out to the east of town, toward the river, then north. Inside Spur's cardboard box stowed in the buggy were some special surprises he had been working on. He came to the oak tree with the yellow ribbon around it and left the buggy and Benson at the tree.

"It's only a couple of miles from here. You wait fifteen minutes, then come up slow. If you hear shooting, come in a rush."

Spur took two tin cans from the box in the buggy and put them in his saddle bags, then rode slowly forward, a rifle in the scabbard and his sixgun in his holster.

He was to go forward a quarter of a mile, through a gate on the left, then follow a small stream for half a mile through a pasture and field to a cabin. Sgt. Benson knew the directions. Spur had discarded the idea of trying to sneak up on them. They knew he would be coming, they would have lookouts. He rode slowly, surely, with one hand on the butt of his .44 and his eyes scanning the trees. Halfway along the creek he saw a man beside a horse. He waved Spur forward, then mounted and rode twenty yards behind him. When he was within fifty yards of the cabin, McCoy spurred his mount ahead, leaped off with the saddle bags and dove into a ditch in front of the cabin. It was two feet deep and would carry runoff water in the spring. Now it was dry. Spur heard a pair of pistol shots behind him but felt nothing. He raised up in the ditch and called toward the cabin.

"Bring the girl out! I want to know she's alive before I bargain," Spur called. There was a silence. The man who had been behind Spur ran from tree to tree until he got behind the cabin. Spur saw no one else in back of him now. He wished he had the rifle.

A moment later the cabin door opened and Fleur stepped out. A man behind her held an arm around her throat.

"Are you all right, Fleurette?" Spur called.

"Yes." The reply was soft, but he heard it.

Spur had been getting his surprise ready. He took one of the tin cans from the saddle bag and made sure the quarter stick of dynamite was well buried in the white powdery substance. He pressed some wadded paper on top of it and put the six-inch length of dynamite fuse and cap into the dynamite. The packet of stinkers was safely in his pocket.

"Well, bargain," a shout came from the cabin.

"All the cash I could get was a thousand," Spur called.

"Two thousand or no more girl."

"Maybe I could raise fifteen hundred," Spur called.

"Bring it in."

"I don't have it with me. It's in a buggy back at the road. I'll have to go get it. Keep your gun-happy people under control." Spur lifted from the ditch and walked to where his horse was grazing. He stepped into the saddle and rode slowly back up the way he had come. Spur expected no sudden rifle shot to blow him off the horse. They did not know for sure who he was. He was the "person" who had been given the ransom note. There wasn't time to connect him with Hilda Johnson. He rode slowly into the brush at its thickest point and quickly swung down from the horse. He was out of sight of the cabin. Spur tied the mount, took both the tin cans in his saddle bags which he looped over his shoulder and then began to run.

He slid like a black ghost from tree to tree, circling to the back of the cabin. When he came close enough, he saw it had a rear door, but no back window. He paused at the side of a tree and studied the whole area. There was no guard that he could spot. No rifle edged around a corner. He checked the tin can bomb he had fixed with a fuse.

Dynamite fuse usually burned at a foot a minute. He had tested this particular roll and found it to be burning a foot in fifty seconds. Those ten seconds could be important. He had a six-inch fuse on the small bomb, so it would burn for twenty-five seconds. It seemed a terribly long time, but since there was no one to see it, it should work. Any shorter fuse would invite disaster. He had seen a six-inch fuse burn in six seconds through some mistake in making the powder-impregnated material.

Now he took out the matches and broke one off, then moved as close as he could get to the cabin in the trees. He paused there twenty yards from the structure and lit the sputtering fuse. Then he ran forward.

Spur placed the bomb on the ground ten yards from the cabin and raced back into the brush, then another twenty yards to be well out of range.

He wasn't sure what would happen. He had chanced on the idea one day and had done only one other test. It had worked marginally well. Now he peered from behind a tall tree and waited.

The fuse burned with too much smoke! If anyone stepped out the back door . . . Just then a man did come out, stared around, saw the smoking fuse and took two steps toward it, then he turned as the bomb went off.

Spur watched in fascination. Most of the white powdery material blasted forward by the dynamite, and the searing, fast-burning flame of the exploding dynamite ignited the tightly compressed cyrstalin white phosphorous. The hot phosphorous burst into immediate flame and burned so hot that nothing could put it out.

A spray of the burning, sticky phosphorous hit the guard, clung to his clothing and in an instant burned through the layers of cloth and began searing his flesh. He screamed in terror and pain as one glob hit his neck and burned an inch wide hole through to his neck bone, slowed as it disintegrated the bone and continued on through to the other side. He fell, his dead eyes still staring in outraged horror.

Most of the flaming phosphorous hit the sides and roof of the cabin. The shingles ignited at once, and within ten seconds the whole roof was a mass of flames. Someone came running out the back door. He looked around and waved. A second man came out, pulling Fleur with him. They both were forced away from the burning building, back almost to the edge of the brush. Spur was now positioned behind a big soapberry.

"Damn, what caused that?" One of the men shouted over the crackle of the flames. The other man shrugged. They backed away from the heat of the flames and Spur reversed his hold on the pistol and slammed it down hard on the side of the closest man's head. He saw the man slump, then brought up the gun aimed at the second man who was working for his pistol.

"You'll never make it!" Spur shouted. The other man dropped Fleur's hand and drew his gun, dove and rolled away. Spur shot him twice as he rolled. The second .44 slug pounded through his broad back, ripped past a rib, through a lung and splattered into five pieces in his heart. He sighed once, then his gun hand opened and the weapon fell out as his head rolled and blank eyes stared unseeing at the sky.

Fleur's eyes went wide and her hand covered her mouth, then she ran into Spur's arms.

"How many men were there?"

"Just these three."

Spur grabbed the sixgun from the unconscious man and tied him with his own belt and kerchief.

"We should be having some company mighty soon," Spur said.

As he spoke they heard a horse coming fast. Sgt. Benson came charging around the side of the cabin his sixgun in hand. When he saw the two men on the ground, he slowed and walked his mount over toward them.

"We need two shots if you're going to explain how you killed that Jasper," Spur said.

Benson lifted his weapon and fired twice into the brush, then swung down. "Any more of them?"

"That's the whole thing. Except for the cabin."

"How did you burn it so fast?"

"I'll have to show you that sometime. Right now I'd suggest Fleur and I get out of here and let the police wind up the affair. You'll want Fleur to make a statement. Come by at your convenience."

Benson nodded. "Seems reasonable. One alive out of three. Got him on kidnapping, assaulting a police officer with a gun, and arson for burning down this citizen's cabin. Should hold him for about twenty years."

Spur and Fleur walked through the woods toward his horse.

"Did they hurt you?" he asked.

"No."

"Did they try?"

"Yes, they touched me, rubbed my breasts. I think they were told not to do anything else. One was soft-spoken, the other two were outlaws of some kind. They didn't talk like they came from around here. They had a heavy southern accent."

"Figures. Maybe they were Friends of the Confederacy."

When they got to the horse she caught Spur's hand.

"Please hold me tight for a minute. I've never been kidnapped before." She blinked quickly but there were no tears. "I don't know how much longer I can be strong and tough."

He held her and kissed her lips and smiled down. "Fleurette, you don't ever have to be strong and tough. I like you just as much when you're soft and warm and loving."

Her smile widened and she reached up to kiss him and when he did her tongue was brushing his lips, then in his mouth. "Would it shock you if I said this whole thing had made me wild to be loved again? I mean, I'd lie down right here, right now, if you want me to, if I could talk you into it."

He kissed her again and when she started to sit down he held her up.

"Sweet little Fleur, I'd love to get your skirts up and your drawers down right now and do all sorts of things with you, but we just don't dare. We have to get back to the office. Now Dr. Larman knows whoever works in that office is associated with you, so I can't use it anymore. I'll probably stay in your room. Or I could just use the hotel side. We'll see."

Fleur nodded, then started unbuttoning the front of her pale green dress. "Sweet Spur, I understand all that, but what would a few minutes hurt? There's no one around and if you don't touch me and kiss me and love me just a little, I'm going to explode. You don't want pieces of me all over the woods here, now do you?"

She had the dress open then, caught his hand and pushed it inside the cloth to her thin chemise. Spur felt the warmth of it as his hand touched her breast. No matter how many times he saw them or touched them, breasts were still a thrill for him. His hand began squeezing and rubbing the softness through the cloth. She sank down and pulled him with her. They sat on the grass beneath the trees dappled by filtered sunlight.

"Oh, yes, sweet Spur, oh yes!"

His hand found its way over the top of the chemise and closed around her bare breast.

"That's so delicious! I feel just warm all over, so wonderful. Oh, it's coming again!" Her hips bucked toward him and then she squirmed over him, lying on top of him and her whole body shook in a long series of jolting spasms that made her vibrate like a lopsided buggy wheel. He kept massaging her breast and knew that he was ready, but he had decided not to enter her, not out here. But damn, he wanted to! His hand brushed down her thigh and her legs spread.

"Come on, Spur, sweet Spur. Just a quick one. I can have my drawers off in no time!"

She caught his hand and pulled it tightly against her crotch. Her hips pushed against his hand, rubbing over it, teasing it.

Spur had to use all of his will power to roll her away from him and stand. He pulled her up beside him.

"Tonight for sure, Fleur. Promise." He buttoned up the top of her dress, then kissed her lips once more and boosted her up behind the saddle. She sat behind him, as they moved out of the brush to the road. Her arms were around him tightly, her breasts, hot even through her clothes, pressed tightly against his back.

As they rode she became more and more excited. It was dark before they got back to town and the hotel. They put the horse away and went in the hotel side. As soon as the room door closed and locked, she held out her arms.

"Now it's my turn," she said.

CHAPTER 12

Oliver Russell was the last person off the train that stopped in St. Louis depot at 5:15 P.M. It came through various connections from Chicago, and he waited for two wide-shouldered tough-looking men to step in front of him before he moved quickly through the station, to a carriage that was waiting for him. The bodyguards sat on either side of him and his male secretary stood outside on the step and held on with one hand as the rig rolled down the street toward the best hotel in town where he had a three-room suite reserved.

Russell seemed small compared to his associates, but he stood nearly five-feet ten, and was solidly built. In fact he had done some bare-knuckled boxing in his youth which accounted for the small scar over his right eye and the slight twist to his nose. Three times surgeons said they had straightened the nose, but each time the bend came back. He refused to pay for any of the operations.

He sat in the carriage in front of the hotel until his secretary had registered all four of them in the suite and two adjoining rooms. Then he went in and up the stairs to the second floor. He never stayed on any floor other than the second, and he never would until Mr. Otis perfected his elevator and they were in widespread use. He had ridden an Otis elevator in 1857 in New York City at the E.V. Haughwout and Company store. Good man Haughwout; looked ahead, the way Oliver Russell did with his Oliver Russell Mercantile and Dry Goods, the second largest retail and mail order business in the world.

He settled in his suite, and waited for Leonard to put away his clothes in the dresser. It was nearly dinner time and he was famished after suffering for two days on the train with atrocious dining-car food.

Russell studied the menu Leonard had brought up made his selections, shaking his head. Absolutely no French dishes at all. What was one to do out here on the frontier? Cope, he decided. At last he told Leonard what he wanted—one whole pheasant under glass with wild rice stuffing and go easy on the thyme. On the side he ordered a large baked potato, curried broccoli and onions, with a very light beef bouillon to start, followed by a green salad. For dessert he ordered cherry brandy and apple dumplings.

"Be sure there is plenty of maple sugar syrup on the dumplings. I don't want it all cooked away."

"Yes, sir, Mr. Russell. When do you wish to dine?"

"Leonard, how long have you been with me?"

"Two years, sir."

"Then you know beyond question that I *always* dine promptly at eight. This should give the slowest kitchen plenty of time. At eight sharp, here in my suite."

"Yes, sir."

When Leonard came back, Russell gave him a sealed envelope and verbal instructions.

"This is to be delivered personally into the hand of one Dr. Isidor Larman. No one else. No henchman. I

113

want you to describe Dr. Larman when you return, so be sure you hand-deliver it to him only."

Russell scowled thoughtfully at Leonard as he left. The boy was learning. Eventually he would move up. Russell tried the overstuffed chair and looked out the window. There was nothing to see except the front of a building across the street. He would miss Martha tonight. She had become a Thursday evening habit with him. He rubbed his crotch without effect. Hell, he'd just have to rough it. He might try the bar or the dining room later on. There was bound be one good looking woman.

He went over to the small desk, opened a briefcase and took out some papers. Projections. Business was down by 1.5 percent and he had to figure out why, and how to reverse it. Eliminate the competition was the most reasonable answer. When he got back to the office, he would figure out some new way to try to buy out Millers'. If he could grab their store at a reasonable loss potential, he could incorporate them as a division and gradually phase them right out of business. Perhaps he could concentrate some types of his merchandise in that store, and give broader display to his other lines. He would think about it. In the meantime, he expected Dr. Isidor Larman to pay him a visit almost at once after he received the note. At least that's what he had suggested. He had the money. Money always talks loudly.

He went to the window and looked down. Yes, as he thought, he saw the small man coming across the street, along with the giant. He had not met Dr. Larman but he had heard of him. Not a nice person—a scoundrel, a criminal some said: but Russell could forgive all that if he only had the diamond! Perfect diamonds had been his one great passion for five years now. He even sold diamonds in his stores. He owned some of the best diamond jewelry pieces this side of New York City.   But the one he had his sights on would be the real "jewel" in his collection. The Star of Pretoria. Nothing could get him worked up like top quality flawless blue-whites!

He shivered for a moment just thinking about it. He did not expect the dwarf to bring it with him, no more than the small man expected Russell to have a sack full of bank notes worth three hundred thousand dollars.

They were both businessmen, shrewd, and consummately careful. Good businessmen. It would work out. He stood with his back to the window when they came in. Leonard knocked, then opened the door. He came first.

"Mr. Russell, I've got Dr. Larman in the other room. He'd like to see you."

"Yes, show him in, Leonard."

Even knowing what to expect, Russell was momentarily shocked at the appearance of the small man. He was much shorter than the merchant had figured, and his head larger. At last he worked up a smile and moved forward, leaning down to shake hands.

"Ah, the famous Dr. Isidor Larman. I have heard many things about you."

"Not all of them good, I trust," Dr. Larman said grinning. He lifted himself into a chair Russell indicated.

"We have some talking to do," Russell said. He saw that Tor, the giant, had stayed in the other room. Russell nodded and Leonard left the room and closed the door.

"Now we talk. You have the diamond, the Star of Pretoria?"

"Yes, in a safe place. Did you bring the money?"

"It's available here, I wired the authorization.

When do I get to see the gem?"

"The sooner the better. Tomorrow, after the banks open?"

"You are a cautious man, Dr. Larman."

"I've found that caution helps one to live much longer."

"It is blue-white and flawless?"

"Absolutely."

"As I read, you had little difficulty in obtaining it."

"There were some problems, and unfortunately more are rising each day. I'd as soon be rid of it and get on about my other projects.

"What might they be?"

"It's impolite to pry, Mr. Russell. They don't concern you or the diamond."

"What time tomorrow, then?"

"Eleven o'clock."

"Where would be convenient?"

"There is a quiet place by the river a few miles beyond town that would be private," Dr. Larman said.

"No, not possible. Why not use somewhere totally public? I would suggest the inside waiting room at the railroad depot. A big open room with many wooden benches. Would that be a good spot?"

"Excellent, Mr. Russell, unless counting 300,000 dollars out to me in public would embarrass you."

"I expect you can estimate the money quickly and quietly by looking in a black satchel I will be carrying. Oh, I will have two highly reliable men with me. Both will have cut off shotguns under their coats. Frightfully effective at close range with double-ought buck rounds."

"The arrangements meet with my approval, Mr. Russell. I too shall have a friend with me. Large and terribly efficient."

They parted at the door.

"We will see you tomorrow then, at eleven," Russell said. He smiled and reached down to shake hands. The dwarf stared at him for a few seconds then nodded.

"Yes, tomorrow."

Russell watched them walk away, the dwarf with his one stiff knee and distorting hunchback. A strange sight indeed—in sharp contrast to the exquisite beauty, symmetry and perfection of the diamond they possessed that he must own.

He waved Leonard out of the room and lay down on the bed. It was large and soft, just as he had ordered. The time was almost six P.M. Plenty of time for a short nap before dinner. Yes, tonight he would dine in style. If only Martha could be with him. . . .

Four blocks away in the Grand Hotel, Spur McCoy had just lifted his lips from a soft, sweet breast when a knock sounded at his hotel-side door.

Fleurette brushed a strand of hair off her naked shoulder and frowned at Spur. "Whoever it is, tell them to go away. You promised me."

Spur lifted away from her on the single bed, pulled his shirt back together and buttoned it as he walked to the door. He had closed off the bedroom behind him and now unlocked and pulled the hall door open.

Sgt. Benson strode into the room, his eyes glowing. "We might have something good," he said.

"You recovered the diamond?"

"No, but we're on to something. I had a man watching you and room 714. While you and I were gone, the giant and the dwarf went calling. A messenger brought them an envelope, then they went to room 202 in the Westerner Hotel. Room 202 is a suite, the most expensive one in town. The man staying there is Oliver Russell, of the Mercantile and Dry Goods house in Chicago. A very big man, with money and contacts, and he's well known as a fancier of precious, unique, and terribly expensive diamonds."

"He's come to buy the Pretoria?"

"I'd bet my brass buttons on it."

"So we must make our move before he gets the diamond, or take it in the process of the transfer," Spur said. "If only we had someone who could get in there and talk to him."

"I've been questioning the staff. He has dinner ordered for eight sharp tonight. He always eats in his room."

Spur started to grin. "I might just have an idea. Isn't he known for being a man with an eye for the ladies?"

"Seems I've heard that, Mr. McCoy."

"Fleur is working in the office. We'll have her bring his dinner to him. It would be my bet that she could figure out some way to talk to him, maybe stay for the evening."

"You're putting her in danger."

"Remember the killer with a knee in the groin? She can take care of herself. Let me go talk to her a minute."

Spur went into the bedroom, caught Fleur's hand and pulled her into the office. He bent and kissed one of her bare breasts as she hugged the open dress to her waist.

"What on earth. . . . ?"

Quickly he went over the new developments. "Do you think you could deliver his dinner on one of those little carts, and get him interested enough in you to find out what he's doing?"

"But tonight you *promised*. . . ."

"The night is not over yet."

She sighed. "Sure, I could wear a perky little blouse and show some cleavage, and act a little saucy, vamp him a little. He's a businessman away from home. . . ."

He kissed her wet lips. "Good girl! I'll get rid of Benson and be right back." He went back into the hotel room leaving her standing, puzzled, pleased, frustrated, yet with a tiny smile on her pretty face.

"What room is your man in?" Spur asked Benson as soon as he got back.

"Two-o-six."

"Fleur will do it. She'll be the serving girl. Can you arrange that with the staff?"

"Yes."

"Great. We have added another piece to the puzzle. If we can grab the stone during the transfer, we can implicate both of them, and you'll make headlines nationwide."

"Yeah—*if*. You tell Fleur to be at the manager's desk at the hotel at 7:30 tonight. Have her wear something—you know, low cut."

Benson rubbed his left shoulder, the one he had a bullet cut out of the year before, and sighed. "This one is starting to get too complicated. A nice simple murder I can understand." He went out shaking his head.

When Spur returned to the bedroom he found Fleur lying on his bed naked, her legs spread and one knee lifted.

"Spur McCoy, I'm going nowhere until you get your pants down or just open your fly and push it in me fast and hard. I've got to have you right now or I'll shatter into a million pieces!"

Spur opened the buttons on his fly and knelt between her soft white thighs. "Baby girl, I'll never tease you. Right now I want you just that bad too!"

He had to open his belt and unfasten the top button of his pants to get himself out, then he kissed her and she put her arms around his neck and held on. He nudged forward, felt the opening and she moaned as

119

he drove fast and hard into her wet and ready hole.

"Yes, love, yes!" She shouted. She climaxed almost at once and he went with her, pounding hard and fast, not wanting to make love, just wanting a fast, hard fuck to relieve his building pressure. She kept climaxing again and again as he built and in less than two minutes he had powered over the top and jetted into a series of bull-like lunges that left him empty, drained and exhausted. He hung over her small body for a moment, than fell to one side and she purred and nestled against him.

"Now sweetheart, I'm ready to take on this Mr. Russell and tease him into telling me everything I want to know."

He couldn't answer her for a moment. He lay there panting and knowing he was dead, but hoping he would come back to life.

An hour later, Spur and Fleur stood in the manager's office at the Westerner hotel talking with Sgt. Benson.

"All arranged. We even found a uniform like the girls in the dining room wear. We'll get one a size small for you and you can do something with the buttons."

"I can figure that out, Sergeant Benson," she said.

"You better come along, miss. The food will be ready in ten minutes, and Mr. Russell has made it clear that he eats *promptly* at eight sharp." The manager led her down a hall toward the employees' section.

"And we're going up to room 206 without any of his people seeing us, right?" Spur asked.

"This is police business, civilian."

Spur grinned. "I'm about as much civilian as you are. Let's go. I'm not going to let my charge walk into a trap like this without backing her up."

"She can foil him if he tries to bed her?"

"She has a trained knee."

Sgt. Benson nodded.

"I'd sure as hell like to know what goes on in that room," Spur said.

Upstairs they slipped into 206 without incident, propped the door open a crack and took turns watching.

"She's coming," Benson said.

Spur edged to the door and looked out. Someone had carried a cart up the steps for Fleur. She arranged things on it, then straightened her uniform, black with white cuffs and ruffles, and an open throat that dipped low. She rolled the cart down the hall, stopped at room 202 and knocked. A moment later she opened the door and went inside.

CHAPTER 13

Fleur saw the door open, and a young man nodded at her.

"Come this way, miss."

She rolled the cart and tried to walk erect, attractively, but then she realized he was not Russell, he was too young. She pushed the rolling cart through a connecting doorway into a second room which was fixed up like a parlor.

A large man sat in an overstuffed chair, going over some papers. He looked at his gold watch, nodded and put the papers away. She pushed the table up to him, opened the leaves the way she had been instructed. Fleur laid out the china plate, cup and saucer, and sterling silver flatware, just as they had shown her, then she stepped back. She had not worn a chemise and had left the top button on her blouse open. It let the cloth pull downward when she reached, and it almost, but not quite, showed the side of each breast.

He looked up at her, and smiled.

"Well, the food looks inviting, and you certainly are a breath of spring breeze as my server. Would you wait a minute while I test everything?"

"Yes, sir," she said.

"Would you take off the lids, please."

She bent over to remove the lids from the covered dishes. She bit her lip a little, but continued to bend low so her blouse fell open more. He probably could see her whole breasts and nipples now. She smiled and looked at him. "Is everything all right?"

He smiled. "Yes, everything looks just lovely. I don't like to eat alone, would you stay please? That will be all, Leonard." The young man nodded and left without any show of surprise.

Oliver Russell settled down to demolishing the pheasant. He ate quickly, without talking. Now and then he looked up at her and smiled.

"The bird is well cooked, just the right spices in the dressing. Compliment the chef for me." He waited a moment. "Would you remove the main course and bring the dessert." he said, prompting her.

She had forgotten, the dessert was on the lower rack.

At once she went to the table and bent forward to remove his plate. He caught her shoulders. "Dear, do you have a name?"

"Fleur."

"Fleur, how nice. 'Flower' in French. A beautiful name and a beautiful girl. You must know that when you bend over that way... I can see your breasts."

"Oh!" she said in mock alarm and drew back.

He chuckled. "Now, now, Fleur, don't overplay your hand—or in this case, your tits. They are fine ones. Let me look again."

She bent toward him, and his hand darted forward. Before she could move it went inside her blouse and captured one warm breast.

"Mr. Russell, you shouldn't!"

"Shouldn't, but doesn't it feel good? Perhaps we should forget about dessert for now." He stood, still gripping her breast and led her to the couch on the far side of the room. He sat down and pulled her beside him.

"Yes, maybe I am rushing things a little." He took his hand off her breast, and drew her to him for a long, warm kiss. She didn't let him enter her mouth. His hands massaged her breasts through the thin blouse. He kissed her again and moved his hand up under her skirt.

"Yes, a good one. I imagine you would want a tip, a gratuity, right?" He looked at her but she didn't say a word.

"Come on, Fleur, how much of a tip?"

Fleur almost panicked, she didn't know what to say. He was offering to give her money for making love! High, make it so high . . .

"Five hundred dollars," she said.

He laughed. "You little whore! I might give you five dollars. Two would be about right."

"And they told me you were some big, important man from Chicago!" Her voice was suddenly angry and snide. "That diamond ring is probably a fake, just like you are."

He looked at the four carat ring set in platinum on his left hand. "My dear, that ring is worth two thousand dollars, *more* money than you'll make in twenty years. I happen to be an expert on diamonds."

"Sure, just like you're an expert on cooking. The cook put twice as much thyme in that dressing to test you. You never noticed the difference."

"You're lying."

"Ask him yourself, I'm getting out of here. Important big spender. Ha!"

He stood when she did. "Look, I don't want to be alone right now. I've got a big deal coming up tomorrow and I need to relax. How about if we start over?"

"You mean you *are* the important, big spender?"

He took a money clip from his pocket and showed her a sheaf of one hundred dollar bills. "If you are extra nice to me, I probably could find one of those hundreds in there for you."

"I said five hundred. Money don't mean nothing to you. To me, it's everything."

"Hey, be reasonable. I came up from five dollars to a hundred."

"Five hundred or no sale."

She took his hand and put it down the top of her blouse, and shuddered as his hand found her breast and began rubbing it. She put her hand on his leg and brushed up toward his crotch. She could see the swelling behind his fly. He was ready!

"Look, it's the principle of the thing. I'm a retailer, I never would overprice an item like this."

She pulled away from him and stepped back. "I don't guess you *are* that big timer. No big deal tomorrow, no nothing, and you won't get me on my back, either."

He stepped up beside her. "Look, you saw the money. I've got plenty of it. And I *am* on a big deal. Tomorrow I'm going to buy a diamond. The biggest, most beautiful diamond I've ever seen. I saw it on display in Chicago last year. Marvelous, beautiful. I have to have it. And I'm paying more money than you know exists."

"Talk is cheap, honey. Damn cheap."

He scowled and walked to the door and back. "I am not just talking. I'm paying three hundred thousand dollars for one diamond.

"Just one little stone?"

"Not little, and not just any stone." He looked around and reached for her breast. She let him touch her. "It's the Star of Pretoria!"

"So?"

"It's a famous diamond, haven't you heard of it?"

"I don't read the papers much, honey."

He laughed. "What the hell am I doing trying to convince some cheap whore...."

She slapped him. He stepped back, amazed. No woman had done that to him in twenty years.

He started to hit her back, then laughed. "Christ, what am I doing? Fine, so you are *not* a cheap whore. At five hundred, you'd be damn expensive."

She stepped away when his hand went up. She buttoned the top of her blouse and frowned. "I don't understand you. First you brag about having money, but you won't spend it. Then this big cock and bull story about hundreds of thousands of dollars. You must be crazy. Yep, that's it. I'm getting out of here."

He caught her from behind, a hand cupping each breast. "Now take it easy. I am a rich man, I just don't like to throw money around. So I was hasty. I'd like to see you naked, pretty little thing like you, do a man's character some good."

"You're weird. You make your big buy tomorrow afternoon and then you show me the stone tomorrow night."

"I am not weird." He squeezed her breasts and she cried out in pain. "And the buy is in the morning. Christ, I should make you come just so you would see. The railroad depot waiting room at eleven o'clock. I'll show you I'm no small-timer. I've never raped a woman in my life but I'm tempted now. You want to get out of your clothes and show me how good you are for a hundred?"

She spun away as his hold relaxed.

"Big timer, I told you five hundred. You show me that big famous diamond tomorrow night here in your room, and you got a deal. I get to wear it while you do me, and you do me for a hundred dollar bill. Deal, big timer?"

She held out her hand and he took it, and shook it. He pulled her close and kissed her and massaged one of her breasts. She pushed him away.

"No freebies, Jasper. You're not in Chicago now."

"Hey, no offense. I'm looking forward to seeing you all naked and panting and wanting it tomorrow night. Just don't get too close tomorrow. You'll see the Star of Pretoria right here, right after you bring me dinner tomorrow at eight."

She adjusted her blouse, folded down the sides of the table and rolled it to the outside door. Then she was in the hall again and pushed the tray to the far stairs and went down without looking back.

When Spur saw the door close, he rushed down the near stairs and across the lobby to find Fleur leaning against the side of the stairs.

"Please get me out of here before I throw up. I'm not used to being called a cheap whore!"

She went in the employees' entrance and came out a few minutes later in her own clothes. Spur and Sgt. Benson took her out the back way, hired a hack and when they were inside, looked at her.

"Did you find out anything?"

"I found out I'm overpriced as a $500 prostitute," she said and laughed. "Those girls really have it rough. I never thought much about it before." She sighed, enjoying the suspense she was building up. At last she giggled.

"He's here for the Star of Pretoria, all right. He wears a two thousand dollar diamond ring and is nuts about diamonds. He says he'll prove to me he's no tinhorn by paying $300,000 for the Star of Pretoria tomorrow at eleven o'clock at the railroad depot waiting room." She shivered and pulled her shawl around her tighter. "I hope you don't mind, but right now I have to get a bath or I won't feel clean for a year."

Benson and Spur made some plans, and then they dropped the cop off at the police station. When they got back to Spur's third floor room, Fleur motioned inside. He unlocked it and she fell into his arms and began to cry.

Spur helped her sit down, held her and after five minutes she had it cried out and sat up gasping.

"Oh, damn! It was unreal. There I was acting like a high class prostitute, and he *believed* me! That's what hurt, I guess. It really hurt. The sonofabitch *believed me.*"

"You're a good actress. Congratulations."

"But I used my body to get information. He had his hands all over my breasts, and I *let* him."

"So what? I use my body every time I knock somebody down. You used your body when you kneed that guy the other day. You use your body when you carry a dummy and stage an arrest. It's not immoral to use your body. Now don't tell me you think because he felt your breasts that it was immoral. Girl, sex has nothing to do with morality. Sex is natural, as essential and normal as breathing and eating. There is nothing strange, unusual, immoral, unprincipled, scandalous, or reprehensible about letting a suspect fondle you a little. You got the information we need and *that* is damn moral."

There were tears in her eyes, and he held her tight.

"You said he wanted you there to watch the buy tomorrow?"

She nodded her head.

"Good, because we're going to keep as many regular passengers out of there as we can, and have a lot of plain clothes policemen in there, including me."

"I still want that bath."

"Right, a bath for you and then I'm taking you downstairs to dinner, a late dinner."

"But...."

"No protesting, it's the least I can do for you after what you did tonight. You should get a bonus from the company. I'll write up the report myself."

"I'd rather you didn't. I don't think Mr. Wood would be much pleased."

"You let me determine that. Now, I'll take you up to your room, order you a tub of hot water and guard the bathroom door until you get there."

All Fleur could do was nod.

Later at dinner, he finished his steak and looked at Fleur.

"You never did tell me how they kidnapped you."

"No."

"I'd like to know."

"Well, it kinda happened suddenly."

"*What* happened suddenly?"

"I was going from the room to the bathroom and the big one, Tor, came out of his door suddenly and knocked me down. When he picked me up, my reticule fell open and my derringer dropped out. He took me back in his room and the dwarf looked through my purse, found the identity card, and decided I was really spying on him. So he sent me out to the cabin with the three hoodlums, sent you a note, and you know the rest."

"You're right, I wish that you hadn't told me. I'm sending a note to the head office suggesting that none of our people carry any identification. It's too dangerous."

He walked her back to her door and kissed her cheek.

"You get a good night's sleep. We have a big day tomorrow."

"What about that other promise?"

"We'll have plenty of time later. I need some sleep too."

He kissed her lips, pushed her inside the open door and patted her soft little bottom.

CHAPTER 14

Spur slept in the next morning, not arising until 7:30. He had a quick breakfast, trimmed his sideburns with a pair of sharp scissors and barber's comb, and put on a soft, wool cap with a bill, a pair of heavy black metal rim spectacles that had plain glass lenses, and a high collared jacket. He didn't think anyone would recognize him. He took a quick ride to the railroad depot and walked through the waiting room. He saw six men who were reading newspapers, obviously policemen.

Outside, Spur spotted Sgt. Benson also reading a paper. He walked up and tapped the cop on the shoulder. Without looking around Benson groaned.

"Damnit, McCoy, I told you we'd handle it!"

"How did you know it was me?"

"Obvious. Too much camouflage. You overdid it. Turn the collar down for a start."

"Your cops inside look about the same way. You've got six of them at precise intervals. Tell some of them not to read the newspaper. Maybe one could be sleeping or some such."

"Yes. I also have two men on each of the hotels ready to follow the players in this little drama. I just hope there won't be any gunfire in the building."

"I'll instruct them on the rules," McCoy said.

"You're getting close to the edge of my patience, Spur."

"Sorry. Keyed up a little. I'm worried. For a man supposedly as careful as Oliver Russell is, why would he slip and tell a woman the time and place of a buy of a stolen gem? He knows damned well it's illegal. Just doesn't ring true."

"That's why I have two men on each of the suspects."

They paced outside the depot, watched three trains come in and discharge passengers. They both walked through the waiting room again and now the police were less obvious because there were about thirty other people in there, seated and walking about.

Spur's pocket watch told him it was 9:30 A.M.

"Going to walk over to the St. Louis Hotel. Isn't far. See if anything is happening."

"Don't get in the way, Spur. This is my baby, and I want to get that diamond back. The whole town is counting on it."

Spur waved, and turned down his coat collar, then walked away.

By the time Spur had walked the six blocks to the St. Louis Hotel, it was nearly ten A.M. He went into a bar across the street and had a beer, came out stretching and staring around casually to see if he could locate Sgt. Benson's undercover police. He found three of them at once—one man with a newspaper on a bench across from the hotel, a second in a chair tipped back on the porch of the establishment, and a third sitting in a hack as if waiting for a fare. None of the men looked the part they were trying to play.

As he leaned against the facade of the saloon, a fancy carriage came wheeling around the corner and stopped directly in front of the four steps that led up to the St. Louis Hotel. A moment later a sturdy man came out and got into the rig, followed by two tall, squarely built men who could be nothing but bodyguards. Another smaller, better dressed man came out, told the driver something and then anchored himself on the step outside the carriage, caught a handhold, and the vehicle rolled forward.

Spur hailed a hack and told him to follow the carriage ahead, but not to be obvious about it. Behind him, Spur saw the policeman come alive and get his buggy in motion.

There was no subterfuge in the man Spur assumed was Russell. He drove straight to the depot, stepped out of the carriage and now Spur saw he was carrying a black satchel. Was it large enough to hold $300,000 in federal banknotes?

Russell and the two guards walked into the depot. Spur guessed it was a scouting trip, a quick run to see if there were any obvious problems they might run into when the delivery time came. Spur strolled to the far exit of the depot and waited. Two minutes later Russell led his team out of the door and walked quickly back to his carriage. Spur ran around the depot a shorter way, and found a cab just as Russell's rig pulled away. Should he follow Russell again? He ordered his driver ahead, giving him instructions each time the other rig turned.

Twenty minutes later they were near the outskirts of St. Louis. It was a quiet street of a few houses and vacant lots. A hill and a patch of woods backed the place where Russell stopped. Spur had kept his rig well back and now he turned in at a house he hoped was vacant. No one came out of the place. He waited and watched. The other rig sat there, waiting.

From behind him, spur saw another buggy coming.

133

It moved quickly, the horse sleek and strong. Fast, Spur thought as it went by. Then he saw a flash of the driver. Tor!

"Back up!" Spur shouted to the driver. "We've got to follow that rig that just went by!"

The cab driver turned around and hurried after the other vehicle, but already it was almost abreast of the carriage occupied by Russell. They had changed the rendezvous. Russell was probably trying to throw off any one following him. He almost made it. He saw Russell get out of his rig and approach the buggy.

Spur kept his driver moving forward, slowly. Now he was close enough so he could see Russell looking at the oncoming rig. One of the big guards came up to Russell's side and Tor stood up in the other rig and shot him with a hidden pistol. A belching roar followed as the second bodyguard fired his shotgun point blank at Tor and slammed him off the buggy seat to the ground. Russell had been handing the satchel inside the buggy when the shooting started. Now he jerked it back and jumped behind the buggy, squatting down. The shotgun blasted again and the top of the buggy turned into shreds, then the horse panicked, and raced away, flying down the road with no driver in the seat. Spur was not sure if there were a live or a dead dwarf in the rear or if no one was there at all.

Spur ordered the driver to follow, but he refused. He stopped the rig and tied the reins, refusing to go near the gunfire.

The big Secret Service man swore at him, leaped out of the hack and ran forward, his sixgun in his hand, wishing he had another one of his phosphorous bombs. Russell stood, saw Spur running toward him, and got into his buggy. He ignored the wounded guard in the ditch and drove away. Spur wondered where the second guard was. Behind him Spur saw another rig coming fast. He drove forward but Russell quickly outdistanced him. He stopped and looked at the buggy behind. It slowed near him and Sgt. Benson looked out.

"Jump on board. What the hell happened? Both my men who were trailing Dr. Larman are wounded, one of them probably will die. My other men lost Russell at the depot but saw you follow him out here. What happened?"

Spur pointed to the wounded man and the giant lying by the side of the road and told what he had seen.

"So we don't know if Dr. Larman is alive or dead. We don't know if Tor is dead nor where Russell's second guard is. And we don't know if Russell got the gem or not. I'm sure he still has his money."

They came to a crossroad. Spur jumped out and examined the tracks in the dust, waved to the right toward the river, and the buggy turned the corner, picked him up and they were on their way.

Sgt. Benson handed Spur a rifle, a Remington repeater.

"Just in case we catch him."

They found the tracks ahead again and Spur saw them go off the road near a stream and then circle.

"He's trying to double back and lose us," Spur said. "Stay on the road and backtrack. Watch the field over there and the trees. No way he can cross that water. I'll get into the woods and try to flush him out."

Spur took the rifle and ran hard and low into the trees, then angled on a course he knew had to cross the buggy tracks. He found them a quarter of a mile from the water. They were still doubling back.

Then Spur cursed out loud. He remembered this area. There was an old cable flatboat that worked across the fifty-yard-wide river nearby. He didn't know if the boat were still functioning or not. But if it were, Russell could get his carriage across after all. Spur settled down to a fast trot following the wheel marks through the soft ground. It had been a year since he had been in this area. The tracks turned left now toward the river. Either the driver or Russell knew where he was going. Had Russell's guard been driving the rig? No, they had a driver on it before the three got in at the hotel.

He came to a slight rise and a hundred yards below he spotted the crossing. The flatboat was still working and was about halfway across the water. Spur charged the rest of the way to the landing, lay on the rough boards and sighted in with the rifle. He knew all along what he would shoot at. He had to slow down Russell, that meant the horse. Spur never liked killing horses, but sometimes it was necessary. He sighted in on the head of the animal. His third shot hit the animal and it went down as if struck by lightning. The operator of the cable crossing came out of a small shack. Before he could say anything, Spur turned the rifle at him.

"I'm with the St. Louis police. Stop the boat, now."

The old man with white hair straggling from under a battered felt hat with no crease and no brim, snorted.

"You don't understand how this one works, sonny. Can't stop her if I wanted to. Force of the water gonna pull her to the far shore, and drag old Bruno up there into the mud if he stops. He knows better, I know better. So we got to let her get across. Hell, you killed the man's horse. That rig ain't going nowhere."

"Bring it back to this side, then."

Again the old man chuckled. "Will, just soon as it hits the far bank and my man on board reverses the cable clamp. That's the way this one works. Not like some of them fancy boats they got on the other rivers."

"No other way to get across?"

"Hell yes, you're strong. Swim over. I used to swim one way every day just to keep in shape. Ain't done it now for a time. Not much current out there now. You should be able to get across and not drift more than half a mile downstream."

Spur looked at the cables again. They hung six feet apart, the lower one three feet out of the water.

"The cables, could I walk across them?"

The old face looked up with a grin. "Wondered when you was agonna think of that one. Sure. Done it myself five, six times. Not as much fun as swimming. Best too if no hombre is gonna shoot at you. Your friend over there might be a bit nicked out at you for killing his animal."

"Could you use this rifle and keep his head down if he tries to shoot?"

"Ain't *my* war, son. I don't hold with killin' and I might miss so much as to unscrew his head. Nope, not my fight. You decide. Swim or walk."

Spur saw the flatboat hit the far side. "How long to get the rig back over here and then cross again?"

"Nigh on to fifteen minutes each way. Course now, son, if I was not wanting you to follow me, I'd sure as hell not let that scow come back."

"Damn. All he has to do is tie up your man, right?"

"Check."

Spur looked at the water. It might be quicker to swim than try the cables. Safer too, but then he couldn't take the rifle. He shrugged, took the rounds out of his pistol and tied it by the trigger guard around his neck on a loop of leather thong. He stripped off his jacket, gave it to the operator and looked across the water. The buggy was where it had been. The flat-bottomed boat had not moved. He saw a man with a satchel run off the dock and into the fringe of woods. He was going upstream, towards St. Louis.

"How far upstream is the nearest bridge?" Spur asked.

"Ain't one."

"Any way to get across?"

"Yep."

"What is it?"

"A bucket on a cable, two miles up. If old Charlie is there today. Used to use it a lot. Little bucket you sit in and it hangs on a cable. Oxen pulls you one way. Bucket on each end of the cable, so someone can go each way same time."

Spur eyed the cold water again, took his jacket back from the old man and reloaded his six-gun.

"I'll take a chance on Charlie. If he's not there I can still swim."

Spur held the rifle at port arms, tied his holster down to his leg and began running upstream. There was a trail of sorts that had once been a road. He made good time and had worked up a good sweat when he saw the land start to rise. Five minutes later he stopped at a small hill fifty feet off the water. The river had bored through a rocky ledge here, leaving cliffs on both sides. On one point he saw the cable and the bucket. There didn't seem to be anyone around. He ran to the bucket and banged on a steel triangle. From below he heard a shout. Spur looked down a steep trail and saw a man fishing.

"Be right up, but it'll cost you a silver dollar," the man said.

Spur caught his breath while he waited. He didn't have a silver dollar. He took out two greenbacks and when the man came up, Spur handed the notes to him.

"Best I can do, does this thing still work?"

"Old Charlie's the name and it damn well better work. Get in the bucket there and hang on. Take you about three minutes to get over. I heard some shooting downstream. That you?"

"Yep." Spur said. He stepped into the steel cylinder.

Old Charlie looked at him with new respect and went out to goad the oxen into motion. At once Spur began swinging out over the cliff, then he was away from the land and looking down at the swirling water. He hoped that Old Charlie wouldn't stop the oxen and leave him dangling in the middle with no way to move either direction. But the rig did not stop. The other bucket passed him at midstream empty.

When the bucket hit the far side, Spur was at the edge of it and he stepped out, grabbed the Remington and trotted along the trail that led upstream. He went fifty yards and turned to the outside, away from the river and soon found what he wanted. It was a perfect lookout and he scanned the area on both sides of the cliff, searching for any movement that could give away Russell's location.

He used an old Indian technique of dividing the landscape up in two dozen segments and worked his eyes over one part at a time, examining it carefully, then sweeping his eyes slowly over the most suspect large area for a trace of motion, than going back to the next section and repeating the process. He found what he was looking for on the fifth segment. Near the river, just upstream of the cliff, was Russell. Spur had hoped that he was in better condition than the merchant. The man appeared tired, stumbling and carrying the satchel tightly in one hand. There was no sign of anyone else.

Spur chose his spot carefully. He decided that Russell would look at the cliff and decide to go around it rather than climb up and then down. He would take Russell just as he came back to the river. By putting two rifle slugs over his head the tenderfoot should panic and give up. Most city people had never been shot at in their lives. The first time was terrifying.

Spur moved to the spot he had chosed and waited. He saw Russell coming after he had circled the cliff. When Russell was fifty yards away, and within ten yards of the water so there would be little place to hide, Spur made his move. He aimed a shot beside Russell, then as the merchant paled and nearly fell down, Spur called out, "Your're surrounded Russell. If you've done nothing wrong, the police won't hold you. So just give up and let's get this over with. What we want is the Star of Pretoria. It's against the law to buy stolen merchandise."

As he spoke, Spur watched the man. He was nervous, surprised, then much calmer. Suddenly he turned and fled. He charged straight for the river. Spur put another round over his head and then ran toward the river himself. Before he got there he heard Russell calling.

"Yes, a wild man with a rifle, trying to kill me! Give me a ride downstream!"

Spur fought his way through a tangle of brush and arrived at the bank just as a rowboat pushed away from shore with Russell sitting beside two young women and a young man. They shielded him and looked back angrily.

"This is the police!" Spur shouted. "The man is wanted for questioning. Bring him to shore at once." But the boat kept going.

Spur thought he heard one of the girls say, "Oh, Pooh!" then they floated downstream, around a bend and out of sight.

Spur stood there watching them go. He could either

run back downstream or swim after them. He could get ahead of them and order them to come to shore. But that brought up a problem. He counted his shots and realized he had only one rifle round left.

What in hell was he going to do now?

CHAPTER 15

Spur turned and ran downstream. He still had his pistol and plenty of ammunition for it. He should be able to run much faster than the rowboat. He would get ahead of them and confront Russell. He would have the people ask Russell to reveal what was in the satchel. That might convince them.

He ran faster, going around the cliff. A new thought struck him. What if Russell had them take him to the far shore and let him off? He ran faster again, wishing now he didn't have the damn rifle to carry.

At last he came around the cliff and back to the river. The current had slowed and he saw the rowboat drifting lazily down the current. He wasn't sure how many were in it. When it came closer, he saw that Russell wasn't aboard. As it came near he called out, "Look, I am a police deputy. Sergeant Benson is on the other shore. We're trying to catch Oliver Russell, the man you just put on the other shore. He's wanted in connection with the theft of the Star of Pretoria, that big diamond. He had money in that valise to pay for the gem. Now please, come over here and tell me if you let him out on the other side and which direction he went."

The people in the boat talked, then nodded. At last they pulled toward his bank. The rowboat nudged ashore and Spur stepped in.

The young man lifted his brows. "He was most convincing. And you *were* shooting at him. We thought we were doing him a favor."

"You were, but unfortunately you may have helped him escape. I didn't *want* to shoot him or I could have. Now take me to the far bank. That is where you let him off, isn't it?"

The man hesitated. One of the girls started to cry. The other girl looked sternly at the young man. "No lying, Jonas, you promised. He asked so we must tell. No, we didn't take him to the other side. He had us stop just around the bend and let him out on the same side. So we should take you back to the same shore we found you on." she hesitated. "He gave us a hundred dollars to lie to you. Right away I knew he must be a criminal after all."

The boy pulled dutifully for the shore, and Spur smiled. Was the girl telling the truth? Was it a trick, a double double-cross? He thought not.

"On the other side you may see a man in his late forties watching the river," Spur said. "If it's Sgt. Benson, you tell him Spur says he's still on Russell's trail. Benson is a police sergeant, so don't lie to him."

Spur stepped out of the craft and heard the shot at the same moment his shoulder was hit and he dove into the dirt at the side of the bank. The boy pushed off with the paddle and the boat was carried downstream.

Spur didn't have time to think how badly he had been hit. The shot had come from slightly behind him. Now he watched that direction. The cliff was upstream from Russell. He had to move either to the right or straight ahead.

Spur had out his sixgun now. He crouched and then sprinted ahead in a charge for a tall tree ten yards ahead. As he ran, he heard one shot from ahead on the river side. Good. Russell was boxing himself in. That was two rounds he had used. Spur guessed Russell had taken the sixgun from the boatman and that he hadn't thought about extra rounds. Six were probably all he had. That now left four.

Spur saw Russell move. He was tired and slow. Spur fired twice and saw one round slam into Russell's right leg and put him down.

A shriek of pain stabbed through the quiet afternoon. Spur let him sweat.

"You had enough, Russell, or do you want me to kill you where you lie?"

There was no response.

Spur put another pistol round into the area where he thought Russell's leg was.

A cry came again, this time long and pain-filled.

"You ready to give up, Russell? I've got forty more rounds. I'll just keep burning them in there until I hit a vital spot. Are you ready to die, Russell? I thought you came down here trying to buy a diamond. Is it worth dying for?"

"No, damnit, no! Just don't shoot anymore."

"Throw out your weapons, all of them."

A sixgun sailed over the brush and landed near the tree. Then a derringer followed and discharged when it hit, but the round blasted into the woods harmlessly.

"Is that everything, Russell?"

"Yes. God, yes."

"Then walk out here, or crawl if you have to."

"I can't."

"Then I'm going to start shooting again."

"No. No! I'll try."

A moment later Spur watched the man stagger to his feet. He hopped on one leg, hanging on to the brush and trees until he came to the clearing, then hopped twice and fell sprawling on his stomach in the grass.

"Stay right there, Russell. Spread your legs and put your hands over your head."

He did.

"You move and you're dead, understand?"

Spur ran up quickly and patted him down, found no more weapons and rolled him over.

"Where's the satchel?"

"Back there. I couldn't carry it."

"Stay still, I'm going to get it. Don't move a muscle."

Spur's eyes never left Russell as he traced the merchant's steps and found the black case. He carried it out and opened it. On top were packets of hundred dollar bills.

"The diamond, you bought it from Dr. Larman?"

"Yes. It's in the bottom."

Mark pushed his hands around the sides of the packets of bills. He'd never seen so much cash money before. Under the stacks in the far end he found a thin wooden case. He pulled it out and opened it slowly. Crushed velvet covered the inside of the box, and lying in the center was the Star of Pretoria, a forty carat wonder. Spur slid the slender case into his inside jacket pocket and smiled.

"Now, Mr. Russell, we have a two mile walk back to that flatboat. I know one boatman who is going to be very pleased to see you."

Spur checked the merchant's wounds. He had one in

the left calf, and a graze on his left ankle. The Secret Service man ripped a strip off Russell's shirt and tied up the bullet wound, improvised a crutch for him and made Oliver Russell walk every step of the way back to the flat-bottomed cable boat. Spur's own wound was a minor graze that just broke the skin.

By the time Spur got there, the boatman had untied himself, unharnessed the dead horse and rolled it off the boat, then with the help of the carriage driver, pushed the rig off the boat.

The ferry had made several trips, and now docked again with Sgt. Benson and his buggy.

Benson stared down at Russell and shook his head.

"They are going to be amazed and disappointed in you back in Chicago, Russell. The stories they will tell about you before you get out of the Missouri State Prison!"

Russell scowled and pointed to the satchel of money. "Now look here, Sergeant. No harm's been done. You have recovered the missing diamond, I had no hand in the stealing of it. I don't know what you can charge me with. Let's say I give the driver of the carriage a hundred dollars for the horse that died, and another hundred for his trouble, and a hundred to the boatman. Then Mr. Spur here will get five hundred for expenses and I'll donate a thousand dollars to the police orphans and widows fund."

"Yes, Mr. Russell, why don't you do that?" Benson said. He held out his hand for the money, which Russell took out of the satchel. He gave Spur five hundred, and two hundred to the hack driver. When he snapped the case shut, Benson took it from his hand.

"I'm sorry, Mr. Russell, we'll have to hold this other money as evidence. You'll get it all back right after your trial. You're charged with receiving stolen goods, assault and battery on a police officer, the shooting death of a giant named Tor, and the deaths of your two bodyguards." Benson smiled.

"He did have the diamond?" Benson asked, looking at Spur.

The government man patted his breast pocket and nodded.

"Now, I think we should take the back road into town," Benson said." I have a nice cold jail cell for you, Russell."

On the way to town, Spur had a quick discussion with Sgt. Benson.

"Look, a few more hours isn't going to make that much difference. What I want to do is let Fleur wear the diamond in her room tonight. What's that going to hurt? She's been a big help in the case, helped capture Jack Houston, and got the details on Russell. We're going to get Houston to turn state's evidence against the others. What can it hurt?"

At last Benson threw up his hands. "I guess you've done most of the work on this one, Spur, and I owe you. But this will even the score. Right?"

"Right, Benson, right. I'll bring the stone around to you first thing in the morning."

Spur dropped off at his hotel and ran up the steps to his room. He closed the door and sensed someone else was there. Then a small voice came from the office section.

"I hope that's you, Spur McCoy."

He laughed. "Sweet little flower, you're right. Come in here. I have a surprise for you. A present that you can wear tonight for as long as you want to."

Fleur ran in from the other room, her practical no-nonsense brown print dress rustling as she ran. He

147

had to smile at the little-girl eager, expectant look on her pretty face.

CHAPTER 16

"A present, you brought me a present?"

"Even better than that, small, pretty, lovable girl." He reached in his jacket pocket. "It's a kind of a present, but only for tonight, all right? It's a very special kind of present. I'd say not a hundred women in the whole world have ever worn something like this, even for one night."

She frowned slightly, then jumped up and down in front of him, excitement spilling over.

He took the thin case from his pocket and held it in front of her. Slowly, with trembling fingers she lifted the lid and looked inside. Her face broke into a smile of ecstasy, wonder, and surprise that made everything worth while.

Fleur looked up at him. "It is so *beautiful!* I've never seen anything so breath-taking. This must be the Star of Pretoria. I can see why men kill for it."

He took it out of the case and put it around her neck. The chain was a little long and the diamond pendant vanished down the open neckline of her dress. She unbuttoned the bodice, spreading the brown dress wide so she could see the gem against her skin. It rested, glittering, between her breasts.

"Oh, I have to see it in a mirror!"

She ran to the glass over the dresser and looked in the wavy reflection.

"Magnificient, delightful, outrageous! I'll *never* let you have it back! Sgt. Benson can go jump in a lake. It's mine!" She giggled. "Oh, it's so *beautiful!* Look! Look how the light sparkles like miniature rainbows. Fantastic, Mr. McCoy!"

She ran to him and threw her arms around his neck, lifting herself off the floor so she could kiss him. Then she clung to him and he brought his arms around her, hugging her to him.

She kissed him a dozen times and then stretched back in his arms so she could focus his face.

"Honey-bear, you know what that does to me, how it makes me feel? I'm all warm and tingly and I want to show you how much I appreciate you letting me wear it. Now that we've got the whole night to ourselves. . . ." She looked closely at him. "We *do* have the whole night to ourselves?"

He kissed her, scooped her up into his arms and he carried her to the bed where he dropped her. She bounced and at once caught the diamond and held it between her breasts.

"You don't know how it makes a girl feel to know that she's wearing a three-hundred-thousand-dollar diamond."

"Show me," Spur suggested as he sat down beside her.

She sat up, went to her knees and caught his head with both her hands, forcing her mouth against his, probing, her eager tongue darting into his mouth, searing him with her heat. Slowly she pushed him down on the bed, still kissing him, stirring his blood to boiling in his veins, rushing to his loins.

She came away and kissed his eyes, then his nose and cheeks. Suddenly her teeth were at his earlobe, nibbling, licking. There was no need for words: each knew it was going to be fire against fire, desire building against desire and passion engulfing both their bodies and minds for as long as their strength held out.

On the way up he had stopped at the kitchen and found three kinds of cheese, some small crackers, and two bottles of the best wine they had.

She sat up, slowly unfastening her dress to the waist. He saw the delicate chemise hiding the twin mounds of her breasts. Suddenly he wanted her more than anything in the world.

She took his hand and brought it to her bosom. "Honey, precious, tonight let's not just . . . just *do* it fast and furious like two starved people. Tonight let's be tender and thoughtful. We are loving and giving and soft and gentle and we'll make love."

His hand brushed her right breast and she smiled. Gently he closed his fingers around it and she sighed so softly he barely heard her. She unbuttoned his shirt and kissed his hairy chest, nuzzling against it, teasing his bud-like nipples. She lay beside him, pressing close, nestling against his body. He put his arm around her and held her, bending to kiss her forehead.

"I just want to lie here a minute, wearing the diamond, close by my man and thinking how delicious it is going to be, and hoping that it will last until the sun comes up, and then until noon if we have the strength."

He held her, moved one hand to her breasts and caressed them softly. They lay quietly for a moment, then she turned to stare at him.

"My uncle warned me. . . ." she began, then she

sighed and shook her head.

"What? Your uncle?" He watched her. She lifted her brows and shrugged. "It doesn't matter. He's an old man and he's probably forgotten all about how young love is." She sat up and let him help her pull the brown dress over her head, then the three petticoats. She sat there with the Star of Pretoria nestled against her chemise and folded her hands in her lap, sitting tall and proud.

"Spur McCoy, I just want you to know that I feel *pretty!* I know it's girl-silly, but with this diamond around my neck I feel like the most beautiful girl in the world!"

He brought half of her long hair around from her back and draped it over a shoulder so it spilled toward her waist. Spur bent over and kissed her lips softly. "Fleurette Leon, you are the most beautiful girl in the world. I've seen all of the girls, and I know. You're the best."

She turned her head and stared at him for a second, then a giggle erupted, shattering her aloof look. She reached for his face, stroking the sideburns, brushing back his moustache, then kissing the tip of his nose.

"Honey, my two ... my ladies feel as if you're ignoring them." She picked up the bottom of the chemise and he grinned and lifted it up. As he pulled it higher he pressed his lips to her soft, exposed belly and kissed upward an inch at a time until he came to a breast. Then he slowed, working around the generous mound, and licking the hot, pulsating nipple.

"Oh, McCoy, you are fantastic! That is so delicious! I wish I could lick you right now. So marvelous. Oh, God, I'm going to break into pieces again!"

A rending climax tore through her slender body, convulsing her, bringing gasps of awe and delight and wonder from her. Twice, then three times the shattering vibrations ripped into her and then she sighed.

"Oh, God, Spur! To think I've been missing this for so long! It's almost criminal. You'd think that my own mother would have. . . ." She stopped, grinning up at him. "No, no I guess not." She looked at him. "You're only half done down there."

He laughed and worked on her other breast until he had the chemise nuzzled above her tits, then she lifted it off.

"I feel so *wild* with my boobies swinging free this way in the open. It's kind of nice, but a little scary. For so long I've been making sure they were decently covered. This must be part of growing up. I *like* it!"

"I'm glad to hear it," Spur said.

She laughed and rolled toward him, thrusting her damp loins against his thighs. "All this, and a half-million-dollar diamond right here on my very own chest! This is a night I'm never going to forget."

He brushed his hand over the slight swell of her little belly.

She caught his hand. "How can I ever tell anyone how that feels? There is no way I can think of. Do it again, the same way. I *love* it!"

He stroked down over her soft flesh, and this time continued downward into her cotton drawers until his hand cupped her mound.

She gasped and reached for his lips. "Damn, but I love to have you doing that and kissing me! It makes me feel hot all over, it makes me want to wiggle my hips and *make* you fondle my breasts and kiss me and just everything."

He ended the kiss and reached for the string ties that held up the drawers. She watched him undo them, then wiggled as he began pulling them down.

"Are you going to. . . ." She stopped and laughed.

"Am I going to what?"

"You won't think I'm nice."

"Fleur, I couldn't ever think you were not nice."

She kissed him quickly and looked away. "I wondered if you were going to kiss my drawers down, too?"

Spur grinned. Why not? His lips went down her stomach and trailed fire, kissing and licking her soft skin, moving downward, working slowly to the line of her drawers, then edging them downward, over her belly and then to the top of her pubic swatch. Fleur gasped.

"Oh, honey, you don't have to," she said, panting, but he knew she didn't mean it.

Spur worked the cotton fabric lower, nestled his nose into the sweet scent of her pubic hair and moaned in delight. He pushed lower, and felt her hips start to move on the bed.

The musky scent of her almost caused him to climax. He pushed farther and lower until he had the drawers down on her legs, which were spread as wide as the constricting fabric let them. Her fingers touched his head, then held it gently as he worked lower.

Spur bent and kissed the red, swollen, moist lips and she rocked in another furious climax. Her hands held him tightly against her crotch until he thought he would suffocate. Gently he pulled to one side so he could breathe. She went from one series of jolting spasms to the next and at last her hands relaxed around his head and he lifted away.

He pulled the drawers off her feet but she didn't notice it. Fleur lay on the bed, arms thrown wide, eyes closed, gasping for air, her heart racing a thousand beats a minute. She looked at him and smiled and then closed her eyes again.

He lay beside her, staring at the Star of Pretoria lying between her breasts. It was the most awesome piece of carbon he had ever seen, and the rapid rise and fall of her breasts accented the picture.

She rolled over and clung to him. "Honey, I never want to be anywhere else but with you. I love you. I love you so much! I want to stay here and live with you and have babies and build a house and have a yard and a dog, and six kids, I want it all so very much!"

He kissed her slowly, tenderly. She kissed him back. He knew it was her passion talking, the power of her climax befuddling her brain. The same thing had happened to him a dozen times. Their soft kiss came again and she moaned and he felt her heat and desire growing again.

"Take me, honey. Take me right now! I need you inside me."

She began tearing at his clothes, pulling off his coat and shirt, jumping up all bare and beautiful and removing his boots, then his pants and falling on her knees in front of his spread legs, cooing and singing to his erect phallus.

He moved and she stopped him. Her lips lowered and she kissed the purple-red head of him, smiled and then jumped on the bed.

"Please, honey, I can't stand it a minute longer!"

He lay on top of her, her furry nest capturing his manhood, claiming it, as if it were some furry animal ready to devour him, its soft lips opening like a delicate flower waiting for a bee. She pressed her hand between their hips, caught his turgid manhood and guided it.

Then neither of them spoke. He slid forward a little at a time, entering her gently as she rose to meet him.

She stretched up and kissed his chest. "I love you, darling," she said, then winced a moment before she whimpered with the unfettered joy of their union.

He glided into her until their bodies met and still he strained forward until she began making small dove-like sounds deep in her throat, sending them both on a fairy-tale ride through the sky.

They meshed together like well engineered gears and she lifted against him with each thrust. After a few moments she stopped him.

"Slow," she said. "Make it last a long time, I want to feel you and hold you inside."

He hovered over her slender form, half lying against her nakedness, half holding himself away. She traced his face with a finger, then kissed his chin and at last his lips.

She touched the diamond and lifted it so he could see it.

"Perfection," she said. "The perfect diamond, and now I'm with the perfect man. What more could a girl ask for?"

Then she clutched at him and they were off again. There was no holding back by either one now as they powered into a long rush of building passions. She broke first, shattering herself on some alien planet millions of miles in space as she clawed at his back with her fingernails, then lifted her legs and wrapped them around his waist.

He filled her with his seed at the same moment with the pounding force of a lightning strike. He collapsed on top of her and she nodded.

Neither wanted to speak, they lay there. At last she untwined her legs and lowered them and he came away from her and held her against him as they lay side by side. He smiled. What a way to start! And they had all night ahead of them, as well as a bottle of wine and three kinds of cheese.

CHAPTER 17

The following morning the Star of Pretoria was recovered by Sgt. Benson, who turned it over to his captain, who gave it to his commander who took it to the chief, who proudly carried it to the mayor who presented it to Mrs. Aurelia Funt. She was overcome with joy and kissed the mayor.

As soon as they delivered the diamond, Spur and Sgt. Bailey took a police rig and drove back to the spot where the meeting had taken place the day before. They searched with a dozen men all morning and at last found the dwarf's buggy. The horse was still in the traces. The front of the rig was splattered with now dry human blood, and the top had been riddled with shotgun fire.

There was no sign of Dr. Isidor Larman.

"We might as well have stayed home," Sgt. Benson said.

"We learned something," Spur said. "The little man isn't dead in the buggy. That's progress. Now all we have to find out is where he is. That's your job. I'll drive the buggy back to town."

"Out of the four on the diamond robbery we have

two, one dead, one not talking. Where the hell is the girl?"

"You went to her hotel room?"

"Checked out, yesterday."

"Dr. Larman's room?"

"She must have cleaned it out for him."

"Like I say, Sgt. Benson, that's all police work. My orders were to get the gem back, and it's back."

At his office in the hotel an hour later, Spur went over the orders he had from Washington D.C. about the President's stop in St. Louis. He would arrive sometime in the afternoon, deliver the dedication speech, and leave the next morning on the same train. There were to be no demonstrations, no large gatherings, no other formal or informal functions attended by the president.

Spur pointed at the instructions which Fleur had read.

"See any problems?"

"A few," she said. "He's staying at the Westerner hotel, which is six or seven blocks from the depot. Will he have his own carriage, or do we furnish one?"

"Wire Washington."

"Then it says the President is to be here overnight. Who is taking care of the hotel security? Us, the other Secret Service men who are traveling with him, or the St. Louis Police?"

"Wire Washington."

He held up his hand. "Enough. There will be five men from our service here in two days. We'll talk about it with them. They must have been through this before."

For the next five days they read the mail, answered telegrams from Washington, showed the new Secret Service arrivals around town, and pointed out a few obvious security problems for the President.

The needed arrangements were all made, mostly by the traveling security guard, and before they knew it the day arrived.

Spur and three of the newly arrived Secret Service men rode up the tracks ten miles to the Soapberry junction where they met the train and were welcomed aboard.

One of the Washington men was George Paladin, a big, strong guy who used his spare time to lift railroad rail sections. "We've got a hell of a lot of surprises for anybody who tries to give us trouble," Paladin said. "We get hit by so much as a rock, you watch that little shed up there on top of that flatcar."

Spur looked over the lashup. It was a nine car train. First was the engine, then the President's private car. Next came the flatcar, followed by three boxcars, and two passenger coaches at the rear followed by the caboose. The boxcars looked different from others, but Spur didn't know why.

Spur sat in the passenger car next to the caboose. It had all the windows raised from the bottom to provide a good firing position in case of trouble, but no problems were expected.

Paladin waved his rifle at Spur. "Hell, I don't know why we bought these. No rumors of any trouble, so we don't really guess there will be any. But you never can tell. That's what we're here for, I guess. Hell of a way to make a dollar, just walking around waiting for trouble."

"What's on the flatcar?" Spur asked.

"Guess."

"I'd say a pair of side-by-side Gatling guns, the six-barrel model, with one aimed to each side of the train. Hope they have the .48 caliber model. They can chew up men and horses like hot butter."

"I didn't tell you what was there, McCoy."

"Going to be a dull damn trip," Paladin said.

Spur knew Paladin had come out of the army and into the Secret Service. He was an action man, best when things got violent and ugly.

The train whistle gave a long, wailing toot, followed by three short blasts.

"Let's move! Trouble! That's the signal," Paladin shouted.

Spur was on his feet. Paladin stuck his head out the window and Spur ran toward the connecting platform of the car ahead.

Before he got there, the window just in front of him on the left shattered as a rifle round bored through it. Spur dropped into the aisle, crawled to the window and looked out.

He saw a dozen horsemen directly across from them, riding hard, waving rifles and pistols. Spur lifted his repeater and shot one man off his horse, then, realizing the train was still moving, he knocked down another rider's horse and aimed at a pistol-wielding man who was not ten yards away.

Spur's first round caught the attacker in the forehead, lifted him off the saddles and smashed him backwards to the ground.

The scream of steel on steel shattered the morning air. The men jolted forward as the brakes clamped on.

"McCoy, keep firing!" Paladin called. "We've got help from up front."

About the same time, Spur heard the Gatling gun firing. The cranker chattered off twenty rounds before pausing. Then another ten rounds came. Spur forgot about the automatic firing weapon and concentrated on the men in front of him. There were more now, ranging up and down the train. One got through the fire from the dozen men in the passenger coach and jumped on the steps between the cars.

George Paladin timed his rush through the door, but misjudged and took two pistol rounds in the belly, then skidded to the floor. Spur turned his rifle on the door and the second the attacker came around the metal frame, Spur put two rounds into his chest.

Outside the battle continued. The Gatling chattered. Spur and the others kept firing, and then the steam whistle blasted.

"Cease firing!" someone in the car commanded. Spur looked out and saw the boxcars ahead of them come apart. The cars pivoted downward to the railroad bank, and twenty cavalrymen charged from each car, pistols blazing as they rode into the confused horsemen in front of them. Now that Spur had a moment to look more closely, he saw that the attackers all had on Rebel soft gray caps. Two of them had been carrying Rebel flags. They didn't know the Civil War was over.

Spur watched as the U.S. blue-coated cavalry swept toward the front of the train, chasing everyone in front of them.

Outside the stopped train, Spur saw three of the downed men lift rifles to shoot. He zeroed in on one and fired, and heard other men in his car shooting too. A moment later the Gatling gun stopped chattering and then there were only the shots of the pony soldiers moving away.

The men inside lay beside the windows, waiting. Then Spur saw movement in the fringe of brush along the right of way.

"There's another charge coming!" he called, and the men reloaded and were back at the windows. Fifty men on foot came out of the brush, rushing from tree to tree, using every rock and depression they could find for cover as they squirmed, crawled and dashed forward.

The riflemen in the last two coaches concentrated on the runners; then the Gatling was free to fire again and it churned dozens of slugs into the area. The Gatlings could fire 200 rounds a minute with a trained gunner and loader.

Spur wasn't sure how many rifles there were in the train windows, but they seemed to have the attackers pinned down. He saw a man behind a rock start to rise, then drop back. Spur had pulled the trigger halfway and he kept the pressure on. When the form lifted again, Spur fired. The round got there a little later, missed his head, but caught him in the groin as he was coming up to a crouch, and rolled him backwards.

The train whistle sounded again, three short blasts, and the Gatling gun cut off. They saw the cavalry charging back toward the second wave of attackers. Spur and his men in the railroad cars stopped firing as the mounted troops boiled over the men cowering on the ground. They were no match for the pony soldiers, and within five minutes the fight was over. Most of the attackers had been cut to pieces, trampled, shot, or captured. Spur went to look at George Paladin. He was dead. Two more in the car had been wounded.

Spur stepped off the train with his rifle fully loaded again and ran toward the front of the train. Two other Secret Service men nodded and went with him. The tracks had been blasted apart ahead, Spur found out, which was why the train had to stop.

A squad of cavalrymen sat mounted on each side of the President's private car. Its windows had been covered with sheets of steel, the vents all came out the sides pointing downward, and there were two guards at the front and rear platforms.

Spur found the chief of Presidential Security, a small, thin man named Kleinman. He was snapping orders. Three men were catching all the horses they could get. Another was tying up prisoners. One man tended to Secret Service and army wounded. Kleinman looked up at Spur.

"You—you're with the St. Louis office, right? You know the way into town?"

Spur nodded. They walked quickly to the first boxcar and looked in. Four men were pivoting a heavy carriage on a turntable so it could be rolled down the steep slanting side of the boxcar to the ground. The men worked efficiently, letting the wagon down against pressure from horses pulling from the other side. Quickly the rig was harnessed with four blacks and driven as near to the front of the President's car as possible. Then six Secret Service men came out of the car with the President in their midst. He was quickly assisted into the coach and the heavy door closed. Extra-wide iron rims on the wheels gave the rig strength and the ability to move through off-road areas. Spur guessed the whole thing was sheeted with some kind of steel plates, strong and heavy.

"McCoy, get a horse and lead this wagon to the nearest road and continue to the hotel. There still is a sizeable force of Rebels out there, so watch for them. Did you see those Rebel hats and flags? I thought the goddamned war was over! You'll have forty cavalry troopers, less any wounded." He turned and checked. "Seven are down, so you'll be working with thirty-three troopers under the command of Major Zackery. We really didn't expect this kind of a reception. It's the closest to the South we have been, but this is outrageous. It's 1869, for God's sakes! The war has been over for four years."

Kleinman nodded at the major who had ridden up.

"Zackery, this is McCoy. He's our local man. Knows the country. He's your guide and he's in charge, he's had military experience, and you'll follow his orders."

"Yes, sir." Zackery looked at Spur. "We're ready to go at your convenience." The Major turned and rode to the head of his command.

"Time to move," Kleinman said, and Spur mounted and rode.

He took three troopers and scouted the way to the road through a pasture across a small stream. One part troubled him. The rumor was that the diamond was to be sold to finance an attack on the President by the Friends of the Confederacy. But the diamond hadn't been sold. The Friends didn't have the money. So how did they get the troops for the attack?

He worried about it for five minutes, then they had a struggle getting the carriage through a soft spot, but after that made the road. Now he put outriders on each side of the carriage—three on each side, and a forward party a half-mile ahead on the road with connecting links. The rest of the men rode around the carriage, protecting it with their bodies and horseflesh.

Spur had six rounds in his pistol and his loaded Remington repeating rifle, but he was uneasy. They were traveling along a road he hadn't been on before, less than a mile from the river, with trees and brush crowding in on both sides. For a while the outriders fell back even with the coach due to the tangle of brush, then they forged ahead. Spur pulled the advance party back and closed in the outriders. He shivered as he sat the saddle of the cavalry horse, carried the rifle across his arms, holding the reins with his left hand. The hair on the back of his neck bristled and he frowned and trembled once more. He had just started to hold up his hand to stop the caravan when the first rifle cracked from the brush to his right and he felt hot lead whisper past his head.

CHAPTER 18

Spur realized the outriders must have been overwhelmed without a shot. Now the main party was surprised and caught on the open road.

"Charge into the trees!" Spur bellowed, and the cavalry troopers fired their pistols at the woods where the shots had come from and charged straight ahead. Spur was slightly behind them, his sixgun useless now until he cleared his own men. He saw one blue shirt careen off his horse, blood spurting from his neck. Another cavalryman fell wounded over his horse and the animal turned and trotted back to the road.

Almost at once they were into the brush and the woods, with trees to help conceal them as they dismounted and dove to the ground.

Major Zackery came into the woods after Spur and kicked off his horse. He came up behind a fallen log beside McCoy.

"It's your command, Major. You know your men."

The West Pointer nodded, then yelled at a sergeant to work four men to the left. He positioned four more troopers to move around the other way, then Spur, the Major and six men moved straight ahead. At first they thought the Rebels had faded into the woods.

Then a sharp volley came, cutting down a trooper, blood gushing from a wound in his head. He spun and fell two feet from Spur, his warm blood splashing on McCoy's hand and his shirt.

Spur crouched behind a tree and peered around. A figure lifted over a log ahead. Spur fired and saw the head jolt backward ad a strip of scalp peeled off.

A wail came from one side. Spur remembered the cloth bag he had brought over his shoulder like a knapsack. In it he had two phosphorous bombs. He pulled out and waved to the major.

"Keep your men back for a moment," he said. "Let me try this little surprise." He had sealed the phosphorous inside the can on this one, and left the fuse protruding. He now slipped a dynamite cap on the end and pushed it into the hole left for it and lit the four-inch fuse. It should burn for twenty seconds. He counted to five, then threw the can as far ahead into the brush and trees as he could. It sailed thirty feet, hit some branches, then a tree, and dropped to the ground. Ten seconds later it exploded with a resounding blast and burning white phosphorous splattered through a thirty-foot circle around the explosion.

One Rebel screamed and stood up, clawing at a glob of the burning material on his shirt. Nobody shot him; the phosphorous burned quickly through his shirt and into his skin. He screamed and fell but it clung to him and ate a hole straight through a rib and into his heart.

Three more of the rebels screamed and ran. The cavalrymen rode them down and moved forward. They charged from three sides into the area and what they found made one young trooper turn pale and throw up.

One of the Rebels had caught a heavy dose of the

burning material, leaving only half of him there, his face gone, all of his clothes burned off, most of one leg and half his torso burned away. Five men were dead in the surrounding area. They chased half a dozen more through the trees, capturing two and killing the other four.

Major Zackery brought his troops and prisoners back to the road. He left a detail to carry the five dead troopers out on their horses. When they rode out of the brush and trees, there were a dozen army rifles aimed at them. The major had left half of his command to protect the President from another attack. Spur looked over the situation, and moved everyone forward. He brought his outriders in and rode. Now he considered it more important to move swiftly than to worry about better protection. He hoped they could get past any more pockets of Rebels before they had a chance to attack.

They continued on the road through the heavily wooded section, came out into a small valley and now Spur knew exactly where they were; about four miles from town.

He called a halt, put out security and then checked through a firing slot about conditions inside the coach.

"The President is fine, a bit shaken by the attacks, but not injured," a spokesman said. "He is thankful for a rest here. He asks how much farther it is to St. Louis."

"Four miles more, all fairly open country, rolling land. We should have no more trouble. We'll be moving again in five minutes."

Spur talked with Major Zackery. The death detail caught up with them, the five troopers tied over the backs of their horses. Three men who had been wounded in the battle were treated.

"It's time we move on," Spur told the Major. "We'll use the same security—three men on the point and three outriders on each side. Let's set a moderate pace and hope nothing more goes wrong."

The major saluted and led the point as they rode down the road that had not been cared for for some time. It was rutted and that slowed them even more, but gradually they came to a better section and the speed picked up.

One of the outriders came in, reporting that he had seen four men riding hard, all with rifles, and all heading the same way as the party.

"They could have been Rebels, but I'm not sure," the trooper said. "We'll keep a keen eye peeled for them, sir." They sent him back to the right flank and the trip continued.

Nothing happened for a mile, then the route went into a small gully, crossed a sturdy but low bridge over a fast-moving little feeder stream, and the road rose sharply on the other side.

Just as the advance guard came near the bridge, it exploded with a crashing roar, sending four-inch planks sailing into the air.

McCoy galloped ahead, saw the situation and moved the President's carriage into a thick stand of brush near the bridge in an easily defendable position. He waited. Nothing further happened.

He left the major in charge and rode hard through the creek and up the ridge on the other side. A half mile away stood a red barn, with its haymow door yawning open. That was strange for this time of year. As he watched, there was a roaring explosion accompanied by a large cloud of smoke, and a kind of fourth of July rocket shot out of the barn door, trailing a plume of smoke. Spur stared at it curiously. If he could see it from this distance it must be huge. He watched in dreadful speculation and saw that it was coming toward the President. He rode back to the brow of the hill.

"Take cover!" he bellowed. "A large rocket of some kind is coming. Get behind a tree—anything!"

He turned and watched, but the rocket was losing speed. It slanted downward and fell a quarter of a mile from him, bursting with a thunderous roar, and then a yellowish green cloud appeared and hung close to the ground. He rode back to the hill.

"Get the President out of here! They have gas shells of some kind. You can ford about a hundred yards upstream—it's a hard, rocky place. Move him now, Major! Right now, before they fire another rocket with more range!"

Spur motioned for two of the outriders to come with him and they rode straight for the barn. They detoured around the growing pall of yellow-green gas near the large crater in the pasture, then rode hard for the red barn. Suddenly Spur knew where he was. He saw the small cabin where Fleur had been held prisoner, now a blackened shell. And through some trees, he saw the big barn.

He directed his two cavalry men into the woods that led up to the barn. It had to be Dr. Larman. Spur wondered how big a defense force he would have around the structure.

CHAPTER 19

Spur had briefed the two troopers as they rode. They left their horses a hundred yards from the barn and worked up silently through the sparse woodland to the near side. They were in back of it and couldn't see the yawning haymow door. A guard at the end of the barn cleared his throat, shifted the rifle in his arms and stared at the woods. The three men stayed still. As the sentry turned to look at the other side of his zone, Spur shot him. The rifle report sounded monstrously loud in the silence of the woods. Spur feared it might bring another guard running, but it didn't. They waited a few moments, then moved up to the edge of the cleared area and looked. McCoy felt in his sack and found the last phosphorous bomb. He just might have a use for it yet. He motioned that he would run to the barn door where the dead guard lay, and that they should both follow him.

Spur checked in all directions, saw no one and ran. Just as he got there, a boy of no more than eighteen came around the corner of the barn, whistling. He had a rifle over his shoulder and the familiar Rebel cap on. They saw each other at about the same time. Spur had been carrying his rifle at port arms as he ran, and now charged another three steps and drove the weapon forward in a butt stroke, catching the boy on the chin, snapping his head back sharply and knocking him unconscious. By the time Spur had the boy's hands tied behind him, one of the troopers arrived and tied his feet. They looked at the door, and Spur motioned that all three would go in.

They edged the huge door open and stepped into the semi-darkness. The far end of the barn was blazing with sunshine, and Spur saw at once that they were in not a regular barn but some kind of a factory. Then he saw the rockets perched on their cylindrical launching platforms at the far end. He also saw two workmen and an angry Dr. Isidor Larman screaming at them. They were changing the angle of the long tube-like launching mechanisms. One of the cavalrymen pointed at himself and the man at the top of the tube adjusting a cable. Spur nodded. He found the second workman halfway up the tube and nodded. They both aimed and Spur fired a second before the trooper did. Both workmen screamed as they fell. The top one was caught by a safety rope and swung back and forth in the air near the tubes.

Dr. Larman roared in anger. Grabbing a torch, he lit one of the large fuses that led to the tail fins of the rockets.

Spur couldn't get a good shot at him. He fired once into the rocket, then charged through the mass of tables and equipment and down a long aisle toward the launching section.

They heard an ear-shattering roar as the big rocket went off. Slowly, then with increasing speed, it shot up the tube and vanished. Spur and the two troopers fired a dozen rounds into the last two missiles without results. Dr. Larman was screaming, firing his pistol and shouting and bellowing. Spur had a clear shot along an opening, and could see both bundles of fuses. Larman tried to get to them with a torch, but Spur fired at him and missed, driving him back behind a large structure.

Three times Dr. Larman tried to light the fuses; each time Spur moved forward came closer to the rockets. At last he was in range.

"Dr. Larman, you better get out of there! I'm going to blow up the last of your inventions," Spur called.

"Idiot! Imbecile! I am the world's greatest scientist! Why do you fight me? Why don't you permit me to build great inventions for all mankind?"

As Larman spoke he edged closer and closer to the wad of fuses. Spur let him move one more time, then, aiming at the arm holding the torch, Spur fired. A scream was wrenched from the dwarf as he dropped the torch and fell, crawling quickly out of range.

Spur fitted the dynamite cap in the white phosphorous bomb, lit a twenty-second fuse with a stinker match, and threw it. It hit and rolled under the mounts that held up the missiles. When it went off, Dr. Larman sceeched in pain or anger, Spur could not figure out which. The phosphorous splattered over the wooden mountings and the inside of that end of the barn, and soon everything began to burn. A gust of wind through the open door fanned the flames and a moment later the furious fire burned through the mounts of the rocket launching tubes, sending them crashing down.

"Out!" Spur shouted. He turned and ran with the troopers at his heels. They barely made it outside before the first explosion went off, followed at once by the second as the payloads in the rocket noses and the dynamite all blew up together.

Spur and the two soldiers were knocked forward by the force of the blast as it burst the roof and walls of the barn into a million shards and splinters, hurling them up to a half mile away. Flames devoured what was left, and then Spur saw the yellowish green fumes and gas, the same they had seen around the first rocket. A farm dog ran toward them barking viciously. It took a short cut through a low spot filled with the yellowish gas. Suddenly the big dog stumbled, then stopped, weaved, looked at them and tried to bark, then fell over and lay still without moving.

"Damn thing's dead!" Spur shouted. "Let's get out of here!" They ran for their horses, mounted and charged back across the fields toward the main road where they had left the presidential party. On the way they saw where the second rocket had hit, far short of the road. They circled the cloud of deadly gas and got to the road, then galloped hard after the dust ahead where the President and his guard must be.

As they rode, one of the soldiers looked over at Spur.

"That little dwarf, you suppose he's dead?"

Spur didn't see how anyone inside the barn could have survived the blast, the fire and the deadly gas. But he had read in the wanted poster that the dwarf had come through other seemingly deadly situations unscathed.

"I hope so," Spur said. "Anyone who would try to kill the president shouldn't be allowed to live."

They caught up with the President's carriage and escort just outside of town. Major Zackery was hoping Spur would come back to lead them to the right hotel without his having to ask a lot of questions.

Spur took over and the President rolled into town, his guards close around the carriage now, through the streets, past the factories, businesses and stately houses, then into the downtown area. Aides said that the President had taken a little nap and was feeling refreshed and ready to see the city. He was taken first to the Westerner Hotel, where the Presidential Suite on the second floor had been prepared. President Grant was whisked in a side door by the Secret Service men and up to his room before anyone knew it.

Spur checked in with Kleinman and was told to be available at all times as a local guide in case President Grant wanted to go sightseeing or to take a ride. They had two rooms on the far side of the suite and Spur waited there. He sent for Fleur, who nodded at Kleinman. He bristled a little, then greeted her by name. When he left, Spur lifted his brows.

"I knew him in Washington," Fleur said. "Now what is there for us to do?"

"Not a damned thing," another man waiting said. He had been nicked in the arm by a Rebel bullet and was supposedly on light duty. He had a domino game going, double twelves, and Spur and Fleur joined in.

An hour later a message came for Spur. He was wanted in the lobby by a Sgt. Benson, St. Louis Police. Spur and Fleur both went down to the first floor and greeted the policeman.

"Hear you had some excitement this morning," Benson said.

"Some, enough to remind me that I don't want to join the army again and go through any more cavalry charges. Those people are crazy the way they risk their lives."

"Yeah, almost as bad as cops, except the army gets all the glory," Benson said. He stared at Spur. "Can we say on our report that Dr. Isidor Larman died in the barn explosion?"

Spur pursed his lips and looked at the chandelier. Then he paced around in a small circle and at last shook his head. "I'd like to say you could, but I can't swear to it. We were close and we escaped. He might have escaped as well. From all the broadsides, he is an extremely difficult man to kill."

"Be hard to hit in a gunfight," Benson said. He was not pleased. "I had hopes you'd seen his scorched little body around the barn."

"Be my guest and take a look. But don't let any of your men sniff that gas out there. Tell the sheriff to put some guards around. That gas is as deadly as anything I've ever seen." He told them about the dog. Benson nodded, kissed Fleur's hand and waved at Spur.

"I better get the sheriff moving before half the county walks into that deadly fog you described."

They watched him hurry out the door. Fleur took Spur's arm possessively. "That still leaves the girl—what was her name?"

"Hilda Johnson, a brunette about your size. Yes, she still could be a problem. Or she might decide to get as far away from this town as she can. I'm sure they'll charge her with murder if they catch her around here. All it would take would be for Jack Houston to testify against her in exchange for a lighter sentence and they would have her put away for twenty years at least."

They walked up the steps toward the Secret Service room.

"Couldn't we wait over at your office?"

"Nope. Too far away. If the President needs us, he will need us fast. But it would be my guess that our illustrious former general and now president is right about now having a nip of brandy and then a nap before dinner. Old army habits are hard to break, and Grant always liked his booze."

"That was just talk!"

"Not so, not so."

As they walked toward the room a woman came out of the Presidential Suite, and moved their way. Too late, he recognized the lady as Aurelia Funt.

She was smiling, with a glow about her that Spur recognized as that first blush of wonder and amazement upon meeting the President of the United States. She looked up and saw them, then nodded at Spur.

"Oh, Mr. McCoy! It's good to see you. I just talked with President Grant. I mean I actually sat there sipping tea and we talked about the ceremony, and about how long he can stay, and what kind of arrangements he needed. He's a fine person, just as regular as any of us."

Spur murmured something.

"It's left me giddy. Mr. McCoy, could you see me to my carriage? I'm so excited and faint, I don't know if I can make it."

He nodded and she took his arm.

"You're a true knight in armor, rescuing me. I just knew I would have to sit down somewhere on the way without a sturdy arm."

He looked back at Fleur and lifted his brows in a "what-can-I-do?" expression. They walked down the hall, and around the corner toward the stairs. At once Aurelia walked more briskly, went past the stairs and unlocked the door of a room. She pointed inside and Spur entered.

"I took a room here just in case I could talk to President Grant. Such a fine man." Mrs. Funt closed the door and snapped the lock. She turned and smiled.

"What a glorious surprise, meeting you in the hall! I'm so excited right now there's only one thing more that would make the day complete." She reached for his crotch and rubbed his genitals.

"Mrs. Funt. . . ."

She frowned him to silence. "Aure, remember?" She took one of his hands and pressed it to her bosom. "Can't you give me a few minutes? I must get to the museum soon." She moved his hand down inside the bodice of her dress until his fingers closed around her breast.

"There, sweet boy, that's better. Yes, and you're starting to grow down here. I hoped you would."

Spur pulled his hand away and stepped back. "Mrs. Funt—Aure—I'm on duty. I'm waiting to learn of any need President Grant might have for me. I'd love to rip your clothes off right here and make love to you, but I don't have time."

She opened the top of her dress and pushed her chemise down, thrusting one ripe, warm breast at him.

"Then just suck me a little, please, darling man."

He laughed, bent and kissed her hot tit, sucked a mouthful in and then chewed on the delicate brown bud of a nipple and felt it enlarging. He gave her one last gentle bite, and came away. Spur stepped to the door.

"It's been nice, Aure, but I've got to go."

"Maybe after the presentation at the museum? After everyone goes we could use the storage room. . . ."

"We'll see. I'm on duty until the President leaves town." He waved, slipped out the door and went back down the hall, hoping that the hard rod in his pants would melt away to normal before he got back to the Secret Service squad room, and Fleur's questioning eyes.

CHAPTER 20

The ceremony at the museum went as planned. Because of the previous attacks, Kleinman made several changes in the proceedings. The president would speak for three minutes, and only in the small auditorium. Everyone who came would be searched, patted down for weapons, even the women. A police matron would do that duty. No more than two hundred persons could attend the presentation.

It caused some trouble for the St. Louis police. Huge crowds milled around outside the museum. They had reserved seats for the large auditorium but were not permitted to attend. One man was arrested. A second man who walked by with a rifle, taking it home from a gunsmith, was also arrested but released when he showed a receipt for the work done on the gun, with the current date, and no rounds of ammunition with him. The police were nervous; the Secret Service men were beyond that. They were alert, worried, and hair-triggered, but nothing else happened.

Inside, after the presentation, they moved to reception, where only forty guests were allowed. President Grant stayed there for half an hour, and had by Spur's count four glasses of champagne and two cookies, then signalled that he wanted to leave and was hurried out a back door into his steel-sided carriage and rushed to the hotel's back door. Spur rode on the back of the carriage, outside, watching everyone. He dropped off at the alley and he and three men swept through it, overturning barrels and boxes, looking for any sniper who might be hidden. They found nothing and waved the carriage in.

Ten minutes later, upstairs in the Secret Service duty room, Spur and Fleur were playing cards. She also had been in the protection detail, her skirt concealing her .44, and a Deringer strapped to her left leg. Now they all relaxed and had a beer and waited. Other Secret Service men were in the hallway—two in the lobby, and two more on each hotel entrance. Any man who tried to come into the hotel with a pistol on his hip was turned away or asked to check his gun in a locked box.

"I think it's going to be a quiet night, and then soon President Grant will be off for Washington and we can get back to normal around here," Spur said.

He went to the door, looked out into the hall and waved at the two security men at the President's door, then at the two further down the hall. All was quiet.

Kleinman stopped by, sweat beading his forehead. He saw the four Secret Service men in the room, and Fleur, and hesitated.

"Miss Leon, due to the delicate situation we have here, I'd be more at ease if you let the men handle the night call on this one and returned to your own room. Would you mind? If we need you we'll send a runner for you."

She stood and scowled at him. "It's just because I'm a woman that you're sending me out, right?"

Kleinman smiled. "Miss Leon, you *are* a woman, a remarkably pretty young woman, and we want you to stay that way. I think it will be best for all concerned if you return to your lodgings for tonight. I'll see you here at 6:30 A.M. to relieve one of the men."

She sighed, stood and put on her jacket, waved goodbye to the men and went into the hall, and down to take a cab back to the Grand Hotel.

Things settled down again. It was just after ten P.M. Spur took one more look into the hall and decided he would have a nap. They had worked out a duty roster; each would take two hours on guard duty inside the room.

While Spur slept, a girl came to the hotel entrance with a covered box. The guards let her by, paying more attention to her cleavage than they did to the box. But it obviously contained only some French pastries, nothing harmful about that, and she said she was taking them to her grandmother in the hotel.

Once inside, she slipped into a first floor linen closet and took off her dress. Under it she wore a uniform like that of the hotel's dining room waitresses. It was black and white, frothy and frilly, but she had left three buttons open so the tops of both generous breasts were clearly visible. She fixed the little white and black hat on her curls and carried the box on a tray into the hall and toward the steps.

A guard stopped her at the steps.

"Miss, where are you going?"

"I'm taking some French pastries to a man on the second floor, who ordered them. I just do what they tell me. Is there a law against it?" She stood close to him so he could appreciate her bosom. It was obvious that she wore nothing under the dress. He grinned, stared at her breasts again and shook his head.

"Just check with me when you come down."

She went up the stairs and to the first turn in the hall. Two more guards with rifles stopped her.

"Yes, miss?"

"I'm supposed to deliver this to the presidential party, courtesy of the management. I hope it's all right?"

The big guard stared for a moment at the fullness of her breasts. His partner chuckled.

"Bert here is amazed at how much tit you're showing. He's really a tit man, loves them."

"Is it all right to go on down?" she asked.

"Huh? Oh, sure." He had edged closer to her, looked down and saw one pink nipple. Goddamn! He swallowed. "Yeah, sure, right this way. I'll walk you down and tell them."

The smaller guard went beside her, staring at her chest. Damn, he had never seen a girl so willing to let you look at her bare boobs! She was something, a knockout. Maybe on her way back he could interest her in a little detour into an unused room along here. Maybe.

He spoke quietly to the guards at the door to the Presidential Suite and they nodded. One knocked and when the door opened, he said something to an aide.

"Go right in, sweetie," the Secret Service man said. "I don't know if you'll get to see the great man himself, but at least you'll get the goodies to him."

She gave him a beautiful smile and stepped inside the door. A tall man in a black suit scowled at her.

"You say this is from the hotel management?"

"Yes, sir. For the President."

"I'm sorry, he's resting now. You just leave it here and I'll see that he gets it."

"Oh, I see." She put on her best hurt kitten expression, blinking rapidly. "Well, all right. I was hoping that I could see the President, maybe say hello."

The tall man in the black suit stepped closer. His eyes looked quickly down her dress front. He nodded.

"Yes, miss. I understand. But do you have any idea how many people want to see the President of the United States? Want to touch him, to say hello? I'm part of the team that helps him get a little privacy."

"What the hell?" a voice shouted from the other room.

A door jerked open and the President of the United States, Ulysses S. Grant, stood in the doorway, bare to the waist, a scowl on his face.

He stared at the aide, then smiled at the pretty girl.

"Well, well, Jeffers, you holding back my pretty visitor?"

"No, sir. I mean, yes, sir. She has something for you."

President Grant walked toward her and the girl shivered. She held out the box, but Jeffers stepped up, opened it and looked inside, pushed one finger all the way through both cakes and then shrugged. He gave the box to the President.

"Jeffers, you certainly do know how to spoil good French pastry!" Now the President saw the girl's bosom and chuckled.

"Jeffers, you may leave now. This pretty lady has simply come to say hello. We owe her a kind word or two, don't you think?"

Jeffers started to say something, then backed away and went through another door and shut it firmly behind him.

The President smiled. "Do you have a name, girl?"

"Yes, I'm Hilda."

"Hilda. Good German name. Are those pastries as delicious as they look?"

"Yes, Mr. President, they are."

He picked out one and took a bite, smiling. "You are right, you are truly correct. Here have some of this one."

She took a bite of it but found it hard to swallow. Now that the time was here, she was wondering. There was no chance she could get away. Even if she got the window open and jumped from the second floor, she might break an ankle or a leg when she hit the ground. Damn, why had she agreed to come? She had been half drunk at the time, she must have been. She stalled.

"Miss Hilda, I'm sure that you didn't come up here just to see me. You had some other reason, didn't you? Almost everyone does. I don't get to talk with the ordinary people as much anymore as I'd like to. Those sonsofbitches this morning showed you why, I guess. But it takes more than a hundred former Rebels to get rid of U.S. Grant! I was Army, you know. I've seen girls around army posts all over this country, some of them showing a little tit like you are, some of them just taking off their dress tops and hanging them out at me. That's hard to walk around when you haven't seen a woman's—face for six months. Now, Hilda, you either take off your dress, or cover yourself up a little. Then I'll know exactly where we stand."

Spur felt someone shaking him; then he was awake and sitting up on the bed in the ready-room and blinking at the tense face of Kleinman.

"Are you awake, McCoy? Really awake? I don't want to have to repeat this. Put on a shirt and come with me. We may have a problem. You know some of the local folks. Do you know of a blonde girl who might want to harm the President?"

Spur buttoned his shirt, stuffed it in his pants and followed the intense man into the hall.

"Someone came bringing a gift of French pastry, compliments of the management, to the President. Jeffers, his aide, had the girl stopped at the door when the old man charged into the outer room. He liked the girl, threw Jeffers out and now they're in there alone. I don't like it."

"A blonde, you said. "Tall girl?"

"No, about five-two, lots of long blonde hair."

"Blonde. It just doesn't ring a bell." Then he thought of the red wig on the railroad car floor. "She might not be blonde. She could be wearing a blonde wig! A brunette girl is in on this plot to kill him, and she's about that size!"

They ran the last few feet to the door. Kleinman knocked and it opened at once. The tall man in the black suit motioned to a connecting door.

"All of us together," Kleinman said, taking out a small caliber pistol. Spur drew his .44 and they poised at the door.

Kleinman turned the knob, held it, nodded, and they all surged into the room at once.

President U.S. Grant stood beside a small table. The rest of the French pastries rested on a silver platter with two sterling silver forks. The President was evidently telling a story, and he looked up with surprise and anger. Kleinman and Spur both had their weapons trained on the blonde girl. Spur looked closer and nodded.

"Hello, Hilda. I think I like you better as a brunette. Lift your delicate little hands slowly."

"What the hell is this?" President Grant roared. "What in the bloody hell is going on here?"

"Mr. President, would you please move slowly into the other room? This girl is dangerous."

U.S. Grant snorted. "Dangerous, hell! She brought me the best little cakes I've ever tasted, and. . . ." He looked up at Kleinman. "You have some information about Hilda?"

"Yes sir, now please back away to the wall." The

President sighed and moved. Kleinman motioned at Spur who edged up behind Hilda, lifted her to her feet and held her arms high over her head. He worked down her right leg through the heavy folds of long skirt, then down the other leg.

"Two weapons, Mr. Kleinman."

"What kind?"

"I'm not sure."

"Take a look, we're all friends here."

The President came forward as Spur lifted the skirt and petticoats. On her left leg he found a .45 caliber Deringer and on her right ankle, a .32 caliber Adams pocket revolver, inlaid with gold scroll work. Spur took them both, and removed the cartridges, then continued his search. On one side under her arm he found a six-inch stiletto.

"Mr. President, we'll have to charge her. We can't let this sort of thing happen," Kleinman said.

President Grant, paced the room, looked at Hilda and turned away. He came back and took one of her hands.

"Girl, did you work out all this deception, this plot, just so you could get in here to kill me?"

"Mr. President, it doesn't make much difference, does it? If I say no, you can prove that I lied to get in, prove that I had the weapons. If I say yes, you'll deal just as harshly with me."

Spur spoke softly. "Mr. President, with the series of armed attacks this morning making newspaper headlines, I think it might be better to gloss over this one, to report it simply as a girl who wanted to see her president so badly that she slipped past guards and tried to win your approval with French pastries."

Kleinman shook his head. "Sir, anyone who is thinking about doing something like this must be shown an example. We must teach her a lesson, throw her in federal prison for sixty years."

The President paced again. He looked at Spur. "And just who are you, young man?"

"Spur McCoy, sir, Secret Service, St. Louis resident agent."

The President shook Spur's hand. "Yes, I remember you in the attacks this morning. You brought in the carriage. I have seen you around and about today. Rockets, cavalry charges, and poison gas. It's been quite a day."

"Mr. President, if I may say one more thing," Spur asked.

President Grant nodded.

"Miss Hilda Johnson is a felon, wanted here in St. Louis for the death of four Pinkerton agents during the robbery of the Star of Pretoria diamond. I can guarantee that she will be jailed here, tried and probably convicted, and given a long sentence for the multiple homicides that occurred as part of the robbery."

President Grant smiled. "Best damn news I've had all day! And we'll simply forget she ever came here tonight. Young man, I like the way your mind works. I may have some more jobs for you one of these days." He paused. "Well, well, get things moving, Jeffers. Mr. McCoy, take your prisoner." The President stopped, walked up to Hilda and lifted off the blonde wig. He let her fluff up her short cut dark curls, and he nodded.

"Hilda, stay a brunette," President Grant said. "I like you much better that way."

Spur grinned, took Hilda by the wrist and led her out of the room and into the hall.

She looked at Spur, then at the guards who were surprised by her transformation from blonde to brunette. He led her down the hall and the stairs and out of the hotel's front door.

She put her hand through his arm. "I won't try to get away. I could have done it, you know. I could have gone down in history as the person who assassinated President Ulysses S. Grant, the eighteenth President of the United States."

"He might have fought you off."

"Not a chance. I would have had my dress off and been behind him and the muzzle would have been against his head." She laughed. "Dr. Larman will never forgive me. I wonder if he survived the explosion at his rocket barn." She grinned and watched him. "You *are* going to turn me in to the police, right?"

"True."

"I just want you to know that when it came right down to it tonight, I couldn't shoot him. Doesn't that win me some votes?"

"Some, but not enough. I'm still going to turn you in."

"When? Does it have to be right now? I mean, here we are, there are dozens of hotels in this town ... What would a few hours later hurt, like tomorrow morning?"

Spur stopped her and looked into her dark eyes. "You really do owe me something after the way you treated me in that house beside your hard-of-hearing neighbor."

"That was a little mean, wasn't it? I could make it up to you. We've got all night."

Spur studied her. She reached up and kissed his lips. He kept looking at her.

"And it will be a long, long time before you have a chance to make love outside of a prison again, won't it?"

"Yes."

"But no matter how hard you try, I won't give you any way to escape, or to damage me, so I can't turn you in to Sgt. Benson in the morning."

She smiled. "The contest will make it that much more exciting then, won't it?"

CHAPTER 21

Spur McCoy sat on the bed and grinned. "So here we are, on the eighth floor. Too high for you to go out the window. I've put a screwed-on hasp inside the door with a padlock and the key is hidden in the room. The skeleton key for the door is also concealed. I've left both my weapons and yours at the desk, so all you have is your sexy little body, and your imaginative mind. Want to play?"

She grinned and sat beside him. "I like the odds. If I win, I get a lifetime of freedom because you'll never see me again. If I lose, I haven't lost one damn thing that I hadn't already thrown away two hours ago."

He kissed her and he couldn't believe how hot her lips were. They seemed to sizzle when they touched his and he pulled her down to the bed, spreading out on top of her, pinning her head to the big bed with a kiss that returned one sizzle for another.

She pulled away and he could feel the heat of her whole body. Hilda looked up at him, a curious, wondering expression on her face, which couldn't disguise the raw passion that hovered there.

"Spur, do *you* like me better as a blonde or a

brunette?"

"It's important to you?"

She moved under him, grinding her hips against his growing erection.

"Yes, important."

He kissed her again, felt her mouth open and thrust his tongue into her moist cavern, exploring it, darting in and out. When the kiss ended, he pushed up so he could focus on her deep, dark eyes.

"I like you better as a brunette; it goes better with your dusky, sexy style, your bedroom eyes, and your slender, enticing little body. But you know the way I like you best?"

She smiled. "How? I think I know. You like me flat on my back, with my knees spread and raised with my clothes all off and you leaning in between my thighs."

"Close enough." He kissed her again, long and hard, then rolled over so she lay on top of him and his hands fumbled with her buttons. She helped him.

"You don't have a damn stitch on under this little uniform do you?"

Her eyes flashed, and she shook her head. "Not one damn, fucking stitch." She watched his reaction. "Look, I can say that word just as easy as men in bars can. It has a nice fucking sound to it, don't you think?"

Spur laughed and parted the top of her black and white uniform, pushing it off her shoulders. Her breasts swayed there in front of him like two downthrust peaks of soft white flesh with fresh pink areolas, centered around brown, pulsating nipples.

"I never argue with a lady who is taking off her clothes." He reached up and kissed the side of her breast.

"Yes, you're getting the idea."

"Lady, quiet. Do you want to be seduced or don't you? I can't get up any enthusiasm for a first class seduction job if you're going to be so damn helpful."

"You want me to fight you a little?"

He shook his head, caught her shoulders and pulled her upward so he could lick her nipples.

"Tits are beautiful," he said. "Nothing like them in the whole damn world." He kissed both breasts and then she was pulling at his jacket, stripping it off him. She was on her knees on the bed then, trying to get his shirt off, her dress around her waist, her breasts swinging like a pair of matched pendulums as she worked at his buttons. He caught her mounds and pushed them together, rubbing them, caressing them like twin jewels. She told him to sit up and she stripped off his shirt, then he pulled down on her dress but she shook her head, sat on the bed and lifted the uniform off over her head. She was right, she wore nothing under it. He had not remembered how slender and sleek she was, with only a little belly over the "V" of black hair at her crotch.

She was woman, she was heat, desire, confusion, lust and sex and wonder all thrown into one. She was near, she was his and she wanted him. Hilda fell on him, pushed a breast into his mouth.

"Darling, let's get out of here tonight. They got the damned diamond back. The Pinkertons knew they were gambling with their lives, they simply lost. Let's get out of here, go down to the waterfront and jump on a boat heading for New Orleans. We can be together all the way down the big river to the wonderful city by the Gulf, and love a dozen times a day. We can know each other in every place and for every reason, and we can team up for the rest of our lives. I'll be good for you, you don't know how good I can be, darlin'. You'll love New Orleans, and I'll make love to you every day, any way you want me to."

She humped her hips and ground them again and again against his. Then she squealed in delight. "Oh, yes, he's growing. I can feel him growing down there! That's marvelous. My titties feel so hot, I think they're burning." She pushed them against his chest then, and he felt her heat sear his flesh and surge hot, steaming blood into his own veins.

She came away from him and bent to his waist, unfastening his belt, opening his fly, pulling at his pants, then moving off the bed and trying to get his boots off. She tugged and tugged so hard it made him laugh. He sat up, pulled off the boots and socks, then let her worm his pants down over his hips and off his feet.

Hilda squealed in fascination, as she jumped on the bed beside him, her hands grasping his erection, pelting it with hot kisses, then looking up at him, smiling and bending her head and taking him into her mouth, gasping for air a moment, then bobbing her head up and down.

Spur knew she was serious. She stopped for a minute and looked up. "I want to taste your juices, darlin'," she said. "I want all of them." She lay on her back then with her head on the pillow and pulled him over her. Her hand held his long shaft at the base so he wouldn't strangle her and she nodded and he began a slow movement. She moaned in rapture and encouragement, and his motion came faster and faster, harder yet controlled, and he knew that he would do it. He knelt astride her, and she saw him reared back, looking down at her from far way and her eyes told him it was all right.

Then it was beyond his control. Some magical switch closed and his mind dissolved, letting his animal instincts take over.

Every muscle in his body contracted, his brain turned off, and his hips jolted forward with a surge that came with a guttural roar.

His hips drove at her again and again as she lay there absorbing his power, accepting his spurting, hot, salty potion and gulping it down quickly.

The lights dimmed, the surge passed and he fell sideways to the bed, only half conscious of what she was doing, not ready to come back to the land of the living until he felt the cord around his wrists. Then he exploded upward, tumbling the girl over backwards, ripping his wrists apart before the knot could be tied, and glaring down at her, naked and shivering on the bed below him.

"If that was your best try, you struck out," Spur said, his mind clearing, his eyes focusing normally again. The face of the girl below was frozen in anger, but gradually it thawed, and she shrugged. "Shit, lost another one." She shrugged again and the grin came back. "At least it was a damn good try, McCoy. You remember that—a damn good try, well timed, just a half of a square knot from successful."

"Sneaky, unpredictable—and a good try." He nodded. "That was one hell of a mouth job. Don't know when I've had one half as good. Damn, but you are one talented lady. Too bad, too damn bad." He held up his hand. "But what is, is, and I can't do anything about it. How far do you think I'd get trying to run with you now that I gave my promise to the President of the United States?"

"You're a federal man, aren't you?"

He nodded. "True. Work for the man who liked your French pastries."

"Yeah, him. Hey, you got a spare hand? A girl could want to be messed around a little bit." She took his hand and put it between her legs. He nodded, moved his fingers up to her softness and rubbed the soft black hair, then trailed down to the center of her and felt the dampness. She threw her head back and her arms went wide apart as her knees lifted and spread and he touched the moist lips to make her wiggle. She smiled, her eyes shut, her breath coming faster.

Slowly he rubbed her, then touched the tiny button. She shivered, gasped, then nodded at him.

"Jesus, Spur, but you are a wonder! Most men don't know nothing about that little number. Jeeesus!" He worked his finger back and forth, twanging her love trigger like a banjo string, bringing a song to her lips.

She moaned a happy tune, and her hips moved, as her breath came in ragged, surging gasps. Spur rubbed her harder and faster and suddenly she broke into a dozen pieces, shattering herself with a pounding climax that sent a million shivers through her whole body, making her feel as if she were on fire, that each of the billion nerve endings in her flesh had just been given a delicate spark of electrical charge, and she vibrated like a precious violin.

Then it was gone. She closed her eyes and shivered, then tried to relax as the spasms came again, slower and farther apart, until she was still.

"Oh, God! Who taught you to do that—some whore?"

He shook his head. "Whores are too busy to teach anybody anything. They do their work and move on. Least, that's what some of the men tell me."

She rested. Five minutes later she sat up.

"How you going to watch me all night, big, naked lawman?"

"You'll be so tired by the time I'm through with you that you won't have strength enough to do anything but sleep."

"You wouldn't bet your career on it, would you?"

"Bet? Wager? Gamble? Not me, lady with two good tits. The only thing I bet on is a sure thing. When we get tired or quit or worn out and I'm ready to go to sleep, you'll sleep too. I know you will, because there won't be anything else for you to do."

"You sure of that?"

"Fairly sure, yes. Because I'll tie you up hand and foot

just the way you tied me in that house of yours."

"You wouldn't!"

"Damn right I would. Now do you want to enjoy your last night of freedom or are you going to let this all go to waste?"

She sighed, her anger cooling, her hard eyes softening a little. "When a girl gets whipped at her own game, she at least likes to get beaten by the best, and Spur McCoy, you are one of the best in the business."

"Truce?"

"Yes, a truce."

"What else did you have in mind for tonight?" he asked.

She laughed. "Nobody is going to ask me what I want to do for one hell of a long time, Spur. I'm just starting to realize that." She blinked back tears. "You ever see one of those pictures some of the sailors have? Those pictures from Japan or China where they show 127 different positions for making love?"

"Almost everyone has seen those."

"What I want to do is go through all those positions."

Spur laughed. "Nobody is *that* good in bed, not in one night."

"Who said one night? You can take a week, a month, if you want, I don't care. I'll stay right in this room with you all the time, and they'll bring in our food, and some clean clothes, and we'll move from one position to the next."

"Tomorrow morning, little lady, we get back to reality."

She pouted. "Hell, you can't blame me for trying!"

"You're a regular Jezebel, aren't you, a frontier Jezebel."

She cocked her head to one side. "I kind of like that. Now come over here and let's get started on those 127. I'm sure that first go-round didn't really count."

Spur nodded and lay beside her. He knew it was going

to be one exhausting night, but he'd been needing something like this for a long time.

CHAPTER 22

It was just past 6:30 A.M. when Spur McCoy turned over the prisoner Hilda Johnson to a smiling Sgt. Benson at the St. Louis city jail.

Benson was full of news.

"We've convinced Jack Houston he should cooperate with us," the sergeant said. "He's agreed to give evidence for the state against Dr. Larman and Hilda for a lighter sentence. I'd say there is absolutely no way we can lose on this one. Of course, we're not sure yet that the dwarf got away. He could have burned to a handful of ash in that fire. But we'll bring charges against him and keep the evidence on file just in case he shows up somewhere else."

The cop looked closer at Spur. "McCoy, you look worn out. This case has really been hard on you."

"Just your imagination, Benson. I've still got a president to get out of town before I can relax." He paused. "Three out of four isn't bad, Sergeant. I'd say you won on that case."

"I'd say we both won, McCoy. Now get out of here and go back and see the President."

Spur tipped his hat to a smiling Hilda Johnson. She managed a wave before Spur slipped out the door and caught a hack back to the Westerner Hotel.

In the second floor Secret Service ready-room, Fleur was bright-eyed and waiting for him. Everyone was talking about the girl who got through security with two guns under her skirts. Spur found a cup of coffee and took Fleur to one side.

"What do we have going here this morning? Any schedule yet?"

"Yes. So far the President will leave at 10 A.M., but Kleinman says there might be some changes. He asked to see you as soon as you get in. He's with the President."

"You mean I'm just supposed to go down there and knock and go in?"

Fleur smiled. "Why Mr. McCoy, don't tell me you're getting nervous about seeing the President?"

He lifted his brows and nodded. "Every time; wouldn't you?" Spur turned and went to the middle door of the suite where the guards were, gave them his name and they passed the word inside. A moment later, Kleinman came out and pulled Spur down to the end of the hall by a window where they talked.

"McCoy, I'm getting nervous about those damn Rebels. If there were a hundred of them here, there must still be a lot more around. We didn't kill or capture all of them. We've made some alternate plans. The President will leave as announced at ten this morning out the back door into the carriage, and down to the train station. We'll drive into a covered section at the north end of the tracks and he will board his special train there. The tracks were repaired and his train brought in about 5 A.M. At least that's the official plan."

"But something else will actually happen?" Spur asked.

"Right. We've got a man in the Service who is about

the same size and weight of the President. He will be the one who will hurry out of the back door into the carriage and into the train. After he's gone, President Grant will leave by the side door in a closed carriage with you driving. You go find a rig and bring it around to that side door at 11 A.M. sharp. A sick man will be helped into the carriage, with his face swathed in bandages. You will then drive four miles east along the tracks to Laneville junction. I'll be on the driver's seat with you. At Laneville the train will stop at just after 11:15. It will wait if we're not there yet. We will have no obvious guards, only you and I and some repeating rifles. Anything else would attract attention. We figure if anyone is going to attack President Grant it will be in the carriage, perhaps with a bomb of some kind."

"It should work. One suggestion. Send along a nurse with the president to add a note of authenticity. I'd suggest you use one of our people, Fleurette Leon. She's in the ready-room. All she would need would be a cape like nurses wear and a black bag for supplies."

Kleinman thought a moment, then nodded. "You set it up with her and get the cape and whatever she'll need. I trust she'll also have a pistol with her."

"Yessir. Two, a .44 and a Deringer."

"Good, now we better get busy."

Spur outlined to Fleur what to get at once. He didn't tell her why they needed it, only to get them within a half hour and not tell anyone why she was getting it. She hurried away looking worried.

Spur ran to the livery and ordered a closed carriage. He settled for a large, enclosed coach, with two seats inside facing each other and a driver's seat high in front. It looked a little like a scaled-down stage coach, except it was lighter built and much fancier. Two horses were needed and Spur had them harnessed up and drove the rig back to within a block of the hotel.

He tied them to a rail in front of a bank, and walked around to the back door of the Westerner Hotel.

Fleur was waiting for him when he got back to the second floor ready-room.

"I found them, this funny cape that nurses wear, and this satchel. Do real nurses wear things like this?"

He took the cape, put it around her shoulders and tied it. He stood back and looked at her, then had her pick up the black bag.

She frowned and stared at him. "McCoy, are you getting me into some kind of trouble?"

"Probably, but I think you'll enjoy it." He looked up at her. "Bandages? Did you get any bandages?"

She grinned. "What would a nurse be without bandages? I got some rolls of gauze, three inches wide."

He stepped up and kissed her cheek. "And you have your weapons?"

"Yes."

"Right. Let's go."

"Where?"

"Just follow orders. Kleinman wants to see you."

They went up the hall, the guards passed the word, and they were ushered inside the door. Kleinman looked at her a moment, and came near to smiling.

"Yes, just the right touch. That should work out well."

A burst of loud talk came from an open door and a moment later President Grant came hurtling through it. He stopped suddenly when he saw Fleur.

"Well, now I didn't know about the nurse!"

"Mr. President, this is Fleur Leon, one of our Secret Service people. She'll go with you in the coach."

"Well, now. Yes, how do you do, Miss Leon? Hell's fire, Kleinman, is all this necessary?"

"We hope not, Mr. President, but better to err on the side of safety."

"Yes, yes. I suppose so. How long until we leave?"

"Burns and I and the rest of the staff will leave with our stalking horses in twenty minutes. Then I'll drop off and come back. You, I, Leon and McCoy will go out at eleven with ten Secret Service men on horses casually in front and in back of our closed coach, but not looking like an escort."

"Oh, all right. How much am I bandaged?"

Everyone looked at Fleur.

"Oh, I'm not really a nurse. But I'd say we should cover one eye and about half of your face. Then wear a hat with the brim turned down. That should do it. You'll want to lean on my arm and maybe someone on the other side. Then you'll appear to be ill."

President Grant smiled. "Yes, this might be an adventure at that. Reminds me a little of the war." He took Fleur's arm and led her into the other room, still talking. She threw one startled look over her shoulder at Spur, who waved.

"I'll go check on my coach," Spur said. "Eleven sharp."

Kleinman nodded, and hurried out to get the fake President dressed and ready to go.

It was nearly two that afternoon before Spur returned the coach to the livery. The operation had gone off without a hitch. No one attacked the President's fake carriage, or the train. Spur and his coach with the real President got through and were ignored by everyone. Spur and Fleur sat in the office part of his quarters, sipping from long-stemmed champagne glasses filled to the brim.

"To your first mission with a President," Spur said. They drank.

"To my first assignment in the field!" Fleur said. They drank. "He was nice. I was surprised. Not rough at all, a perfect gentleman. I was tremendously impressed with our President."

They smiled at each other. "It's been an experience working here with you, Mr. McCoy, sir."

"What's the formality all of a sudden?"

"You didn't read the mail. My uncle says he's proud of me and that I can stay here for a six-month tour."

Spur put the glass down. "Your uncle? I don't understand."

"Oh, dear, I wasn't supposed to say that." She frowned and looked away. "Pretend that you never heard it." He was standing beside her then.

"Your uncle. . . . and he assigned you. . . . You mean you're related to General Halleck? He's the guy who usually assigns people, but I know he doesn't have any brothers or sisters. So that only leaves. . . ."

"William Wood, the director of the Secret Service," she said. "Yes, he's my uncle. I didn't want you to know."

Spur almost choked on his champagne. He had been bouncing into bed with the niece of the big boss in Washington. She could blow the whistle on him and he'd spend the rest of his government duty on a far outpost in the deserts of Arizona somewhere.

"You look like you just had lunch on rattlesnake," she said.

"I probably did."

"You mean us? Us, those delightful times in bed?" She walked up to him and put her arms around him and kissed his unmoving lips. "Hey, you're my boss. I can't send a wire unless you tell me to, right? I wouldn't dare reveal anything about your personal life that had no bearing on your duty, right?" She kissed him again. "And I'm not about to tell good old Uncle Bill anything that happened here between the two of us. He'd order me back to D.C. in about ten seconds. So you see, you're safe with me."

She dug out a telegram and showed it to him. He read it quickly.

> MCCOY. AS OF THIS DATE LEON IS ASSIGNED PERMANENTLY TO YOUR OFFICE AS LOCAL ST. LOUIS AGENT. YOU CONTINUE TO DO ALL FIELD WORK OUTSIDE CITY AND IN WESTERN HALF OF NATION. ANY PROBLEMS WITH HER, LET ME KNOW. LEON NOT TO BE INVOLVED IN ANY DANGEROUS ASSIGNMENTS. (HER MOTHER WOULD KILL ME.) CONGRATULATIONS ON RECOVERY OF DIAMOND. HOPE PRESIDENTIAL VISIT GOES WITHOUT INCIDENT."

Spur put it down. "When did this come in?"

"Yesterday. You've been busy. Oh, there was another important wire."

It lay on his desk under a paperweight over a hand-lettered sign that said: "IMPORTANT!"

"TROUBLE IN SOUTHERN COLORADO. TAKE NEXT TRAIN TO DENVER. CONTACT OUR DROP THAT CITY FOR DETAILED INFORMATION AND NATURE OF PROBLEM. AUTHORIZED TO DRAW $500 EXPENSES AND TO REQUISITION NEEDED SUPPLIES, HORSES, AND BACKUP TROOPERS FROM DENVER ARMY POST. LEAVE ST. LOUIS AS SOON AS POSSIBLE. MORE AT DENVER."

"You're going to be busy, so just one small goodbye kiss or two." She unbuttoned two fasteners at the throat of her dress and when she peeled back the fabric he saw a gleaming, sparkling gem at her throat.

"The Star of Pretoria?" he said with a gasp.

She laughed. "Almost. That nice jeweler friend of yours brought it by. It's a copy in quartz, but he wanted you to have it for helping keep him out of trouble."

"Thank God!"

He took her hand and led her into the hotel section of the rooms.

"I'm starved," Spur said. "First we'll have a late dinner, or lunch or whatever they call it now, and then we're going to come back up here and spend a gentle, peaceful afternoon making love before I leave for Denver. Would that interest you?"

"Everything but the food."

He took off his coat, and turned into the bedroom.

"We can always have dinner later," Spur McCoy said, and fell onto the soft bed with Fleur in his arms.